The Automobile Girls at Newport

"The Automobile Girls" Were Fairly Started.
[frontispiece of the 1910 edition]

Aunt Claire Presents

The Automobile Girls at Newport

or

Watching the Summer Parade

By Laura Dent Crane

Laboratory Books
Astoria, Queens

Publisher's Note

This book is a piece of history. It was first published in 1910 by the Henry Altemus Company of Philadelphia. The text, presented here unabridged and unaltered, reflects the language and attitudes of its time. For more about this and other aspects of the historical background, please see the introduction to this edition ("A Note from Aunt Claire").

The original front cover is printed on the binding of this edition.

Laboratory Books LLC, 35-19 31st Avenue, No. 4R, Astoria, NY 11106
www.laboratorybooks.xyz

First Laboratory Books edition
10 9 8 7 6 5 4 3 2 1

ISBN 978-1-946053-00-8

Library of Congress Control Number: 2017942046

Text set in Egizio URW

Printed in the United States of America

Contents

A fashionable motoring costume of the early twentieth century, as illustrated by the famous poster artist Edward Penfield

A Note from Aunt Claire

The book you have in your hands, the first in a collection of books I would like to introduce you to, is about a lot of things. Friendship and jealousy, which you'll find in any story worth its salt; runaway carriages and slippery jewel thieves, which are a bit more uncommon. Most of all, this book is about adventure. The girls you are about to meet, the main characters of our story, set out to find adventures. They succeed magnificently, of course, and they end up having an enormous amount of fun along the way. If adventures and fun-having bore you, I advise you to put down this book immediately. But if you've ever wondered, even for a moment, what it would be like to strike out on your own, just you and a few chosen friends, to see what the world has to offer—then you've come to the right story.

From the very first page, you'll notice that the girls you meet, though familiar in many ways, seem more than a little odd in others. You see, if these girls had existed in real life, they'd be about 125 years old today. This book, as well as the others I'll be presenting to you (in a collection I am modestly calling Aunt Claire

Presents), were written over a hundred years ago, and many things were different then. In those days, most people still lived without electricity, girls rarely went to college, and women in America weren't even allowed to vote. Girls couldn't do many of the things they wanted to back then, at least not in real life. But in books, things were a bit different. In books, girls got to have all sorts of adventures, adventures that are just as exciting today as they were back then. And so I thought I would introduce you to some.

In case the large car on the front cover didn't tip you off, our first story—the very story you hold in your hands—has to do with automobiles. One automobile, to be precise, and the group of girls who drive it. *The Automobile Girls at Newport*, written by one Laura Dent Crane, was first published in 1910 by the Henry Altemus Company, a publishing house that put out roughly thirty series for young people in the first few decades of the 1900s. The Automobile Girls series, six books in all, follows the adventures of four girls, one aunt, a selection of boys who pop in and out, and a beloved red automobile by the name of Mr. A. Bubble. Ruth Stuart, the owner of said auto, is the only daughter of a rich widower, and, luckily for our story, Mr. Stuart lets his daughter have her way in most matters. Ruth, an adventurous spirit, decides she will travel the country in her automobile with a group of her closest friends: Grace Carter, Barbara Thurston, and Mollie Thurston, with Mr. Stuart's sister, the excellent

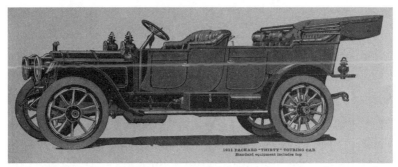

The 1911 Packard Thirty touring car, from an advertisement in the Saturday Evening Post

Aunt Sallie, to serve as chaperon. Aunt Sallie is a long-suffering woman, oddly fond of the color violet, who likes to claim that she is only along to keep the girls out of trouble. There have been rumors that she enjoys adventuring quite as much as any of the girls; but if she asks, you certainly didn't hear it from me.

What you have to understand is that series like this one—stories about girls who go on adventures—didn't always exist. They sprang up in the early 1900s, suddenly and unstoppably, not unlike certain varieties of mushroom after a fresh rain, and they did so for two main reasons. One, that people at that time were absolutely fascinated by new technologies like automobiles and radios and moving pictures, a fascination that spilled over into the fiction of the day; and two, that people were getting around to realizing that girls like adventure just as well as boys.

Since this book has to do with automobiles, we had better start with those. In the early 1900s, automobiles were new enough that they were still quite glamorous and still quite expensive. Everybody wanted to ride in an automobile; everybody longed to own one. Most people couldn't, of course; there were some less expensive models intended for young working men, but they were still beyond the means of most families. Not to worry, though: anyone could read about automobiles any time they liked, because publishers had been busy adding them into stories left, right, and sideways.

Now it was a dirty business, riding in an open automobile on the mostly unpaved roads of those days. For a woman, at least, it was thought to require a heavy coat called a duster (a name that speaks for itself), a motor veil, and goggles. The goggles were so unsightly they were sometimes "accidentally" misplaced, the driver preferring to risk dust in the eye than to abandon fashion entirely. And the fact of the matter was, none of it really worked anyway, so that by the time you got where you were going, your outfit might still be ruined and your skin coated in an unappealing layer of grime. You might rub a protective "vanishing cream" on your face before your journey, and cold cream on your face afterward to lift away the dirt, but even they were ultimately powerless in the face of such an accumulation of dust. What it comes down to, all in all, is that anything more than a quiet ride around town was considered unladylike. Which meant that in the years before our story starts, driving automobiles (like so much of what was fun in those days) was mostly the domain of men.

*Motoring veils and scarves in a 1912 Sears,
Roebuck and Co. catalog*

A 1912 advertisement for Pond's Vanishing Cream

Which brings us to the second reason for the appearance of these books: girls were getting restless. You see, just around that time, the women's rights movement was really picking up speed. More and more women were talking about going to college and having careers and even capturing that highest of prizes, the right to vote. Girls, growing up with all of that around them, decided they might want those things too, but they weren't quite old enough yet. So for the time being, they would content themselves with adventure stories—the type boys had been reading for years, only this time, it would be girls having the adventures.

Of course, girls hadn't been entirely without adventure stories before then. Books called dime novels had existed since the mid-1800s, and some of those books included stories about adventure-having, pants-wearing girls like Hurricane Nell and Calamity Jane. But girls were often discouraged from reading such books, because many families considered them trashy and maybe even a little dangerous, Jane and Nell taking too many risks and wearing entirely too many pairs of pants. And even the girls who did read them may have had trouble picturing themselves in the roles of those parent-less young ladies who were forever shooting pistols and riding horses from one town to the next.

What girls wanted was adventure stories about girls more like them, and publishers, swept along by the growing women's rights movement, decided to give them their wish: in books, at least, girls were camping,

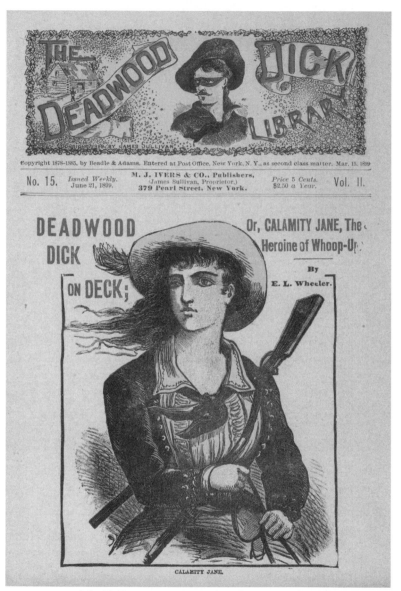

A half-dime novel featuring Calamity Jane

THE AUTOMOBILE GIRLS SERIES
By LAURA DENT CRANE
PRICE, $1.00 EACH

Girls as well as boys love wholesome adventure, a wealth of which is found in many forms and in many scenes in the volumes of this series.

1. THE AUTOMOBILE GIRLS AT NEWPORT; or, Watching the Summer Parade.
2. THE AUTOMOBILE GIRLS IN THE BERKSHIRES; or, The Ghost of Lost Man's Trail.
3. THE AUTOMOBILE GIRLS ALONG THE HUDSON; or, Fighting Fire in Sleepy Hollow.
4. THE AUTOMOBILE GIRLS AT CHICAGO; or, Winning Out Against Heavy Odds.
5. THE AUTOMOBILE GIRLS AT PALM BEACH; or, Proving Their Mettle Under Southern Skies.
6. THE AUTOMOBILE GIRLS AT WASHINGTON; or, Checkmating the Plots of Foreign Spies.

An advertisement for the Automobile Girls series, from the back pages of another book published by the Henry Altemus Company

girls were heading off to college, girls were working in the movies and on the radio, girls were sailing boats and piloting planes, and, of course, girls were driving automobiles, going where they pleased and leaving the boys behind. Suddenly girls were the ones stopping runaway carriages and thwarting thieves, using brains and a fair bit of muscle as well. Girls, for once, were the heroines.

A question does linger, though, as questions often do. Were our girls really free-spirited adventurers, every bit as capable as boys? Or were they still, at their essence, the girls of the stories of old, fainting and wilting and entirely unsuited for anything outside of the home? Our books tried to have it both ways, the result a most

Suffrage parade, New York City, October 23, 1915

curious soup indeed. Girls bested boys on one page and needed their help desperately on the next; girls—even our own Automobile Girls—longed to vote in one book and went about mocking suffragettes in another. It was like the books couldn't decide how much power their girls should be allowed to have.

You will also find, as you turn the pages of these books, a curious mixing of different kinds of stories. Danger and excitement are tangled up with the details of the girls' summer dresses, sometimes on the very same page. You could say, I suppose, that the books are a bit indecisive—a bit unsure of what they want to be. But I see no harm in that. After all, without those asides and pauses and flights of fancy, you might as well be reading a technical manual on mushroom hunting.

And take it from someone who knows: unless you're in the business, such books are really quite a snooze.

But how, a persistent soul might ask, *could a person who cares about a silly thing like bonnets care just as much about something serious, like the catching of burglars?* Well, consider Barbara, whom you will read about shortly. Over the course of the story she gets mixed up with a runaway carriage, a cliff-top rescue, and more than one mysterious theft, and she handles herself with courage and intelligence—and yet, in the midst of it all, she longs for pink hair ribbons.

Now Bab herself seems perfectly happy with this state of affairs, and so am I; and I rather think that anyone who isn't perfectly happy with it is, to borrow a phrase our girls like to use, a stuck-up goose. It's plain as day that the girls in our books—some of them, anyway, and I'm willing to bet some of the boys as well—cared about *both* the automobile ride to Newport *and* the outfit they would wear when they got there. And what an excellent thing to have such fun with both.

But it wasn't all roses and tea cakes and jewel thieves, and we can't let the excitement and adventure distract us entirely from some of the fundamental differences between that era and ours. For one thing, as you can see from the cover, the girls in this story are all white—and so is almost everyone they know. Today this seems odd to us, but it reflects the facts of that time: if the communities these girls lived in had existed in real life, they would very likely have been composed only of white people. And for another thing, people of different ethnic groups and social backgrounds—gypsies, for instance—are sometimes treated as stereotypes, instead of individuals in their own right. Of course, the books didn't invent this way of thinking; they simply reflected the way society was back then. A hundred years ago, unfortunately, this kind of stereotyping was common. So it bears remembering that these stories are from a different time, and must be taken with several generous pinches of salt. And who knows? Perhaps when we read about a time with such different values, and characters who were good and kind but still blind to their prejudices, we might find ourselves wondering what people a hundred years from now will think about us.

And now I believe it's time for me to stop yammering on and let you get to the tale. Just one final word: for those who prefer their adventures with a little less dust to the face, I've selected a less automotive book to introduce to you next time, one that's all about the school days of a girl named Grace Harlowe and a few of her closest chums. And oh the adventures they have! *Grace Harlowe's Freshman Year at High School*, the next book in our collection, brings us a heated award contest, a fairy-like godmother, a most unpleasant math teacher—and even another jewel thief. But all that is for another day. For now, we've got Ruth and Bab and Mollie and Grace, and that beloved auto, in all his bright red glory. So get your motor veils on and have your cold cream at the ready—you never know who you may meet.

The Automobile Girls at Newport

CHAPTER I

Barbara to the Rescue

"Pink hair ribbons!"

Barbara Thurston's brown, bright face seemed to twinkle all over, as she clinked a yellow coin on the marble top of the little sewing table.

"Silk stockings!" chorused Mollie Thurston gleefully. "Wasn't it the luckiest thing that the hotel people wanted so many berries this year!" And she, too, sent a gold piece spinning over the smooth surface. "But, perhaps, we won't be invited after all," she sighed.

"Nonsense!" rejoined Barbara energetically. "When Grace Carter says she'll fix a thing, you can wager she will. She's known Ruth Stuart for three summers now, and she's told us we'd be invited to Ruth's party this year. I can read the invitations already. The only thing worrying me was what we'd wear. Now the strawberry crop has turned out so well, and mother's a brick, and will let us use our money as we wish—I think we're fixed. Then—who knows?"

"I am sure Ruth Stuart's lots of fun when you get to know her," interrupted Mollie eagerly. "If Cousin

Gladys wasn't boarding at the hotel with her, we'd have met her long before. Isn't Gladys a stuck-up goose? Never mind. We'll have the laugh on her when she sees us at the party. Let's be de-lighted to meet her. I should love to watch her when she is fussed!"

"After all," mused Barbara, thoughtfully, "her father was in partnership with papa. It's mighty funny that uncle got all the money. I wonder——" She stopped playing with her gold piece and gazed thoughtfully out of the sitting room window at the hot, empty, yellow road that ran so near the tiny cottage.

Barbara Thurston was sixteen, Mollie just two years younger, and nearly all their lives had been spent in that little cottage. John Thurston, the girls' father, had died suddenly when Mollie was only three years old.

He had been at that time in the wholesale clothing business with his wife's brother, Ralph Le Baron, and was supposed to be a rich man. But when his affairs were settled up, his brother-in-law, the executor, announced that a very small interest in the business remained to Mrs. Thurston. He hinted, darkly, at stock speculation on her husband's part, and poor Mrs. Thurston, overcome by grief, had not wanted to question deeply.

She, herself, happened to own the little cottage, in Kingsbridge, in which she and her brother had lived as children. Acting on his advice, she settled there with her two little girls, and had remained ever since, subsisting on the small income her brother regularly transmitted to her from her dead husband's tiny business interest. Le Baron and his wife, with their daughter, Gladys, usually spent the summer in Kingsbridge, at the one "summer hotel" in the place; but intercourse between the two families had come to be little sought on either side. Kingsbridge was a quiet little village in New Jersey, and, except for the summer visitors, there was little gayety. Gladys Le Baron, especially, had shown herself icily oblivious of the existence of her younger cousins, Barbara and Mollie.

These two were delightful examples of self-reliant young America. Barbara, the elder, looked a regular "nut-brown maid," with chestnut hair that never would "stay put," and usually a mischievous twinkle in the brown eyes beneath the straying locks. But there was plenty of genuinely forceful energy stored away in her slim, well-knit young body, and her firm chin and broad forehead told both of determination and intelligence.

Her sister, Mollie, was fair, with lovely curling blond hair, and a quaint drollery of speech that won her many friends. Both sisters had grown up quietly, helping their mother about the house, as they could afford no servant, going to the village school, and, when they wanted anything beyond the plainest necessities of life, earning it.

This summer both had set their hearts on "really-truly" party clothes, not "hand-me-downs." Their friend, Grace Carter, daughter of Squire Carter, the village dignitary, had promised them invitations to "the event of the season," the party to be given by her friend

Ruth Stuart, a rich Western girl who quite recently had come to spend her summer at Kingsbridge. And didn't Ruth Stuart live at the same hotel with Gladys Le Baron, the snobbish cousin?

To meet the enemy on her own ground, and to have the fun of a party besides, was certainly worth picking strawberries for, thought Barbara and Mollie. So they scoured the country round for the sweet wild ones the hotel visitors liked best. Now each of the girls was fingering gleefully her twenty-dollar gold-piece that meant many days' work in the past, but pretty dresses in the future.

The prospect was too alluring for Barbara to spend much time in wondering about the real "why" of their fallen fortunes, though the question had come to her before, and would again. Now she was ready to join Mollie in eager planning as to "just what they'd get."

"Go get a pencil and paper, Molliekins, and we'll set it all down," she laughed.

Mollie went into the further room and Barbara waited, eyes absent-mindedly fixed on the yellow stretch of road.

Suddenly she became conscious of a curious pounding. There was a queer, wild rhythm to it, and it seemed to be coming nearer and nearer.

Barbara put her head out of the open window. She could see nothing but a cloud of dust far down the road. Yet the pounding sounded louder every moment.

Then she knew. The noise came from the furious

feet of runaway horses. And they were coming past the house with their helpless, unknown victims.

What could Barbara do? Her mother was asleep upstairs and there was no man about the place. There was no other house near. Besides, the slightest delay might prove fatal.

All this seemed to flash through Barbara's brain in a second. She knew she must act. Swiftly and easily as a boy she vaulted the open window, pausing only to snatch a closed umbrella that leaned against the sill. How glad she was she had forgotten to put it away in the closet when she came in from the shower yesterday!

In an instant the girl sped through the gate and out into the road, opening her umbrella as she ran.

There she paused, squarely in front of the approaching dust cloud, very near now. She could hear the click of the stones, cast aside by the flying feet of the horses, and she caught a glimpse of two black heads, wild-eyed and foam-flecked, through the whirling dust.

Barbara strained her eyes to locate hanging bridles. But meantime, swiftly and mechanically, she was opening and shutting the big black umbrella.

"If they'll only stop!" she murmured.

And they did. Fear-crazed already, their legs trembling after a terrific run, the horses dared not seek encounter with that horrible bat-like creature that seemed to await them.

Scarcely five feet away, their wild pace broke. They hesitated, and Barbara flung herself forward and seized the dangling bridles. For a moment she pulled on them with wrists of steel, but it was not necessary. The horses drooped their weary heads and gladly stood still.

Then, and only then, Barbara glanced at the carriage and its occupants.

It was an open four-seated carriage, and in it were Ruth Stuart, Grace Carter, Gladys Le Baron and a strange young man somewhat older than the rest of the party. The girls were leaning back, with closed eyes and white faces. The young man was staring straight ahead, with a blank expression, fear depicted on every feature.

Barbara dared not leave the horses even now. "Mollie! Mollie!" she called.

Mollie was already out of the house. From the window, terror-stricken, she had seen it all.

"Get the girls out," Barbara directed. "I can't leave these brutes, though I guess they're all right now."

In the meantime, Grace and Gladys had opened their eyes. Mollie now stood at the carriage step, her hand outstretched.

As they recognized their rescuers, Grace's pale face lit up. Even Gladys, for once, tried to summon a gracious and grateful smile.

"We're all right, Mollie," spoke up Grace, "but I think Ruth has fainted. I'll help you get her into the house."

Suddenly the young man started up. "I beg your pardon," he remarked in a smooth, pleasantly-modulated voice, "but you really must let me help. I have been utterly helpless so far," and his glance wandered admiringly and a trifle shamefacedly toward Barbara.

In an instant, he had sprung over the wheel and gently half lifted, half dragged Ruth Stuart off the seat.

As her feet touched the ground, she too opened her eyes, only to close them again with a shivering sigh. Grace was at her side in a moment.

"Try to walk to the house, dear," Grace urged. "It's only a few steps."

Mollie took the place of the young man, and, between the two girls, Ruth stumbled to the gate.

The young man stepped up to Barbara. "Can I help you?" he ventured, looking at the now quieted horses.

But a cold voice sounded from the carriage, where Gladys still sat. "I think you might think a little about me, Harry," she exclaimed.

The young fellow bit his lip and hesitated.

"Please," broke in Barbara, "please take her to the house. I can't get these horses and this carriage through the gate. It isn't big enough. But I'll hitch them to the fence and stay with them for a few minutes. You must need rest, all of you!"

Harry Townsend bit his lip as he caught the sarcastic inflection in Barbara's last sentence, but did as he was directed, and walked slowly toward the house with Gladys.

Left to herself, Barbara led the horses, still attached to the carriage, toward the fence, and hitched them by the reins in a clever way all country girls know. "Good boys! Poor boys!" she murmured, petting them, for they were still shivering pitifully with fright.

For several minutes she stood talking to them. Then Mollie's anxious face appeared at the door, and in a moment she stood beside her sister.

"What shall we do?" she asked. "Miss Stuart is feeling very ill, and wants to go home at once. She and all the others refuse to step foot into that carriage again— and I can't blame them; but, you know, it's two miles to the hotel, if it's a step, and we haven't a telephone. Grace says Ruth's father would send the au-to-mo-bile,"— Mollie pronounced the word with reverent care—"but what's the quickest way of getting the message to them? Mother suggests running over to Jim Trumbull's and seeing if he'll hitch up and drive to the hotel. But it's half a mile to his place, and he's very likely to be away anyhow. What do you——?"

Barbara interrupted her decisively. "I'll just drive those horses back to the hotel myself, Mollie Thurston," she said calmly.

"Barbara, you can't! It's risking your life!"

"Nonsense! There isn't an ounce of spirit left in the poor, frightened things. I guess I haven't broken Jim Trumbull's colts for him without knowing how to handle horses. You go tell Miss Stuart that her automobile will be here in two shakes of a lamb's tail. And see, Mollie," the twinkle shone in Barbara's eyes, "of course they'll give me a ride back in the auto!"

Laughing at Mollie's protests, the plucky girl untied the horses and turned them carefully.

"Stand at their heads, just a minute," she cheerfully directed. Then Barbara gathered up the reins and climbed up to the high seat.

"Drop anchor, Mollie," she called, and trotted slowly down the road behind the quieted blacks.

CHAPTER II

Lost, Strayed or Stolen

"**M**ollie Thurston, has Barbara driven off with those awful horses?"

It was Grace Carter who spoke. She had reached the doorway of the cottage just in time to catch a glimpse of the departing equipage.

Without waiting for a reply, she turned from the open door to the group inside just as Mollie rejoined them, exclaiming:

"Barbara is driving the runaways to the hotel for the machine!"

Mrs. Thurston started. She had been downstairs for some time helping to make the victims of the accident comfortable. She was a slim, sweet-faced little woman, whose entire world lay in her two lively young daughters, in whom she had unlimited faith.

But, in a moment, she smiled and said, "I am not afraid to trust Barbara with anything."

Ruth Stuart's lately pale face was glowing. "I think that is regularly splendid of her!" she exclaimed, with more animation than she had shown since she had left the carriage.

"Oh, Barbara is used to taking care of herself," Gladys Le Baron interposed with a supercilious smile.

Mollie looked at her cousin a moment. "Yes," she answered steadily, "we think it is a pretty good thing in our family."

Gladys flushed, and had no reply ready. Ruth looked surprised and Grace plunged into the breach.

"Oh," she tried to murmur off-handedly, "Barbara and Mollie and Gladys are cousins, you know."

"And you never——" Ruth turned to Gladys, then stopped and smiled. "Well, it's awfully jolly to have met you all in this nice, informal way. Grace has often spoken of you," she said.

The girls had to laugh at this, so Ruth continued: "I'm well enough now to be proper and conventional, I suppose. I believe you know I'm Ruth Stuart. Mrs. Thurston, Mollie, have you met Gladys's friend, Mr. Townsend?"

The young man came out from the corner near the window, where he had been seated, and bowed gayly. Ruth nodded in a satisfied fashion.

"There, doesn't that finish it?" she sighed. "The rest of you are all acquainted, aren't you? Now, won't one of you, please tell me why those awful horses aren't running still? I know some horrible white hay-caps started them, and Jones fell off the seat, and now we are here. Who stopped us?"

Everybody turned to Ruth at once. "Why, Barbara stopped them," Grace managed to say first. "Barbara——"

A gay laugh sounded in the doorway, and Barbara herself appeared before them.

"Now I've caught you!" she cried merrily, her bright eyes sweeping the circle. Then she turned to Ruth with a mock curtsey.

"Your ladyship's chariot waits," she declaimed, then continuing in quick explanation: "You see, your driver was scarcely hurt and he rushed back to the hotel at once and sent the automobile along the road where he had seen the horses disappearing. Before I'd gone a quarter of a mile, I met the machine with the chauffeur, and doctor and Jones himself. We sent Jones back with the horses, though they weren't bothering me a bit, and I came back in the automobile. How are you feeling?" and the bright voice softened sympathetically, as she noted Ruth's pale cheeks.

For answer the girl arose quickly, and held out both hands to Barbara. "You're a brick," she said simply. "I fainted, like a goose, and they've just told me what you did. I am so glad I know you, and I guess my father will be glad, too—not to say thankful! Now, please won't you and your sister dine with us to-morrow? No? Make it lunch; then I'll see you sooner. I won't take no for an answer, because I have a very important plan. Dad decides as quickly as I do. So if you'll only say yes—but

I can't tell you about it now. Perhaps, if I make you curious, you'll be more interested when the time comes!" Ruth laughed mischievously.

"What have you up your sleeve now, Ruth Stuart?" asked Grace, curiously. "I never saw such a girl as you are for chain-lightning projects!"

"You'll see," laughed Ruth. "You're in it too, you know. You must be one of my lunch party to-morrow. I know you and Mr. Townsend have another engagement, Gladys, so you will pardon my delivering my invitation before you. Now, I won't say another word.

"Come," she continued, addressing the party, "we must be off at once. If the news of this runaway circulates through the hotel and reaches either your father or mine, Gladys, they'll be wild with fright. Good-bye, Mrs. Thurston, and thank you. You've been awfully good to us. As for you two"—holding out her hands to Barbara and Mollie—"wait till tomorrow at lunch!"

Drawing the two Thurston girls with her, she stepped outside the door and to the gate, the rest of the party following. The machine was waiting in the road, and out of it hurried the hotel doctor toward Ruth.

"Aren't you hurt, Miss Stuart?" he cried. "I would have come in, but Miss Thurston said she would go in first and see how you were."

"I'm perfectly well, doctor," smiled Ruth. "It's too bad you had to come way out here. I hope father will not hear you have been sent for!"

She patted affectionately the nearest tire-rim of

the big automobile. "Bless the 'bubble's' heart," she murmured. "He wouldn't run away with his missus. Barbara, Mollie, this is my best friend, Mr. A. Bubble. I think you'll get better acquainted with him before long. I wish you could come with me now, but I'm afraid neither you nor 'Bubble' would be quite comfortable. And you three must get along well together from the start."

The doctor helped Ruth into the big red touring car and Gladys and Grace followed. The two men and the chauffeur crowded together in the front seat.

"Au revoir," chorused the autoists, and "see you tomorrow," nodded Ruth emphatically to the girls. Then, in a whirl of dust, the big machine sped out of sight.

"Isn't she a dear?" burst forth Mollie, as the sisters turned to go back to the house. "How her eyes shine when she talks! I wonder if I could do my hair that way. I was sure she'd be nice—but what do you suppose she means by that plan? Barbara, for heaven's sake, how did you happen to think of that umbrella stunt? It was great, but you did look so funny—like a sort of desperate, feminine Darius Green with his flying machine! No wonder you stopped the horses!"

"Oh, I heard of a man who stopped a stampede of cattle that way out West once," Barbara answered abstractedly. There was a puzzled look on her face. "Mollie," she said abruptly, as they entered the house, "you didn't take our money with you, when you went into the bedroom for pencil and paper?"

"Why, no," replied Mollie wonderingly. "It must be over there on the table now. I remember I noticed it as I came into the room. I wondered, for a second, why you'd gone away and left it so near the open window. That was before I looked through the window and saw what you were doing. It must be there," and Mollie hurried over to the window.

The next moment she turned an astonished face to her sister. "Barbara!" she exclaimed, "it isn't here, anywhere!" Indeed, the marble top of the little table was absolutely bare. There was no sign of either of the gold pieces.

"Let's look on the floor," said Barbara, quietly. "One of our guests may have unconsciously brushed them off."

Both girls stopped and began a careful survey of the carpeted floor, under the table, and near the window. Their search was unrewarded.

"Let's look in the grass outside," suggested Mollie. "You might have brushed them off as you went through the window."

"But didn't you say you saw them on the table, when you came back into the room and found me gone?" queried Barbara, thoughtfully.

"I was sure I did," Mollie replied. "But sometimes one remembers imaginary things. And if the money had been in the room when I came in, it would be there now. I'll ask mother——"

"No, don't," said Barbara quickly; "at least, not yet."

Mrs. Thurston had gone into the kitchen directly after her return from the gate, and had heard none of the conversation. "There's no need to worry mother about it now. Of course we must find it somewhere. Money doesn't walk off by itself. We'll go out and look in the grass under the window."

On hands and knees the girls worked through the closely cropped grass underneath the sitting room window. Not two days before, they themselves had clipped this bit of lawn with big shears, and it was so close that there seemed no possibility of anything being hidden in it. Certainly nothing was to be found. The girls even looked over the short path, and ground near it. "Your skirts might have switched those small things a long way," observed Mollie, wisely. Yet, as before, the result was—nothing.

Giving it up, at last, the girls sat down in a little garden seat at one side of the tiny yard, and looked at each other ruefully.

"I am so glad I feel sure Miss Stuart will invite us to her party, now," commented Mollie dryly. "Our new gowns and the pink hair ribbons and the silk stockings will be so awfully fetching! But where, where, where, by all that's mysterious, can those double-eagles have flown?"

Suddenly she looked curiously at her sister. "Barbara, you are thinking of something!" she exclaimed. "Have you any nameable idea?"

"No," said Barbara, quickly; "it isn't nameable."

"All right; you never would talk when you didn't want to," complained Mollie. "And I know you want that money back as badly as I do. Tell you what—I'll say the fairies' charm. Don't you remember the one the old gypsy woman taught us? Wish she were here to say it for us! She promised to do all sorts of things for me when I found her in the field with a sprained ankle and helped her back to camp. Why! why! Barbara, this is *uncanny*—she's coming now!"

In truth, down the road a queer little bent figure was seen approaching. "I know her," continued Mollie eagerly, "by that funny combination of red and yellow handkerchiefs she wears on her head. Do let's go and meet her and tell her—it can't do any harm."

"What nonsense, Mollie!" laughed Barbara. But she followed her younger sister, who had already started down the road toward the quaint, little, gaudily-turbaned dame.

Between them, the girls brought her into the yard, Mollie meanwhile busily explaining their predicament. "You'll help us, won't you, Granny Ann?" she coaxed childishly. "You said, that time that I helped you home, you'd always be near when I wanted you."

Granny Ann sat on the garden seat, looking gravely down at the half-laughing, half-serious girls huddled at her feet.

"I knowed," she began in a high, cracked voice, "I knowed my little fair one," lightly touching Mollie's curls, "would need me to-day. Far away I was, when I heard the shadow of her voice callin' out to me—and miles I have traveled to reach her. Granny Ann is thirsty, and she has had no food since morning." The old woman looked reproachfully at her listeners.

Barbara's eyes twinkled at Mollie's rather crestfallen face, when the sybil voiced this most human request. But she said cheerily: "All right, Granny; supper isn't ready yet, but I know mother'll have something." Then Barbara hurried into the house, the gypsy dame waiting solemnly until she reappeared, a moment later, with sandwiches, doughnuts and a big glass of milk.

Granny Ann smiled, but she didn't speak until the lunch had quite disappeared. Then the old woman rose impressively. "There's one sure magic for fetching back money that has gone," she declaimed. "Because you have been good to me, 'Little Fair One,' you and your sister, I will say the golden spell for you." With her hands crossed, Granny Ann began to croon dreamily:

Gold is gladsome, gold is gay,
Here to-night and gone to-day,
Here to-day and gone to-morrow,
Guest of joy and host of sorrow.
Gold of mine that's flitted far,
Forget me not, where'er you are.
Mine you are, as Pluto wrought you,

Mine you are, whoever's sought you,
Come by sea or come by land—
Homeward fly into my hand!

Three times Granny Ann repeated this. Then, with a queer dignity, oddly assorting with her variegated raiment, she turned to the girls. "It will return," she said; "now, I must go to my own people."

"But I thought you said you came here for us by yourself!" protested Mollie.

The gypsy dame drew herself up. "I travel not alone!" she said, stiffly. "Good-bye."

"Oh, good-bye, and thanks ever so much, Granny Ann!" cried both of the girls.

But Granny Ann did not turn her head. Barbara looked at Mollie, her eyes dancing. "The blessed old fraud!" she teased; "her people decided to camp somewhere about, and she thought she'd come over for a call and a lunch, and whatever else she could get! I believe she actually expected us to cross her palm with silver for saying that little rhyme. But I wish I knew really——"

All at once a faint chug-chug sounded in the distance. In a moment a big red touring car appeared, enveloped in dust. "Why, it looks like Ruth's car!" exclaimed Mollie, excitedly. "Yes, I do believe that young man seated beside the chauffeur is the Mr. Townsend who was with them. Barbara——"

But Barbara was walking quickly toward the gate. A moment later the automobile stopped before it, and Harry Townsend stepped out.

"Miss Thurston," he began, soberly, "have you lost any money?"

"Oh, yes!" burst out Mollie, who was just behind, before Barbara could speak; "two twenty-dollar gold-pieces! We've hunted and hunted. We had them this afternoon——"

"Then these must be yours," said the young man, extending his hand to Barbara. In it were two golden double-eagles. "When the young ladies were getting out at the hotel these were found on the seat, and Miss Stuart was sure you had dropped them out of your pocket, Miss Thurston, during the few moments you were in the machine. I am very glad to be able to restore them to you."

"Yes," said Barbara, "but I——" Then she stopped. "Thank you, Mr. Townsend," she said, giving him a clear, direct glance. For some unknown reason the young man's eyes wavered under it, and he climbed hurriedly into the automobile. "I am very glad," he murmured again.

"Miss Stuart expects you to-morrow," he added quickly, and the machine backed round and hurried off.

Barbara stood looking at it, the money still in her hand. But Mollie was laughing happily. Then she saw Barbara's face. "Barbara, what is it, dear?" she demanded. "You look exactly as you did before Granny

Ann appeared, and I asked you if you were thinking of something. What is it? Can't you tell me?"

Barbara shook her head. "It really isn't anything, Molliekins. I did have an idea in my head, but I must be mistaken somehow. You are sure you saw the money on the table after I left the room? It must have been there, then, when the crowd from the automobile came in. I thought I saw some one standing near the table with one hand resting on it, when I came back and called out: 'Now, I've caught you!' But I must not think anything more about it. Please don't ask me any questions. Let us just be glad we have the money back. It is queer, though. Mr. Townsend says the money was found on the seat. I wonder who found it, and whether it was found on the front or back seat? Let's ask Grace. I don't understand it. But he brought the money back, and he's Miss Stuart's friend. Of course we will keep quiet, you and I, Mollie, whether the money was lost, strayed or stolen!"

"Well, I am sure, Barbara Thurston," Mollie answered a little indignantly, "I am not likely to talk of what I know nothing about. If there is any mystery about the disappearance of that money, I am sure you have left me utterly in the dark."

"Don't be cross," said Barbara, putting her arm in Mollie's. "But do you know if Mr. Townsend is a special friend of Gladys's?"

Mollie shook her head. "How should I know?" she said. "Let's go in, it's nearly dark."

CHAPTER III

Ruth's Perfect Plan

Wonderment over the mystery of the money, and excited anticipation of Ruth Stuart's luncheon and "plan," kept the Thurston girls from getting to sleep very early that night. They awoke bright and fresh next morning, nevertheless. Just before eleven they started on their two-mile tramp to the hotel. They were hardly out of sight of the house, however, when what should they see but the now familiar red car speeding toward them. "Look—yes, it is!" cried Mollie. "Ruth herself is making it go!"

The young driver waved a free hand for a second, as she neared them, then wheeled in a broad turn and stopped. "I was so afraid you might have started," she protested tactfully, "for it is such a fine morning for a nice leisurely walk. I was so anxious to see you that I simply couldn't wait, and I told Dad I'd take the 'bubble' and spin out to meet you. Now, won't you please hop in, and ride back with me?"

The girls "hopped" with delighted celerity, and Ruth turned back to them for a moment. "I have reams to talk about," she continued, "but, to tell you the truth, I want my father to be with us, when I begin. So, now, if you don't mind, we'll just ride."

Neither Mollie nor Barbara will ever forget their first ride. "I felt as if I had chartered my own private flying machine, and I was sure the angels were jealous," Mollie confessed, naïvely, at lunch.

They reached the hotel very quickly, and after a cosy chat on the private balcony belonging to Ruth's tiny suite of rooms, found themselves seated around a little table in a cool, palm-shaded corner of the big dining-room. Between them, opposite Ruth, sat big, blue-eyed, open-hearted, Robert Stuart, Ruth's "Dad."

Robert Stuart had made his fortune out West, in the mining country. That was how he started, anyway. For years, now, he had lived in Chicago, buying and selling real estate in the vicinity. There his wife had died, and there his eighteen-year-old daughter Ruth had spent nearly all her life. During the summers she had traveled more or less, and the last few years had frequently gone East. Her father's sister, Aunt Sallie Stuart, had brought the girl up since her mother's death, which had occurred when Ruth was a little girl. Aunt Sallie was not present at the luncheon, because of a bad headache. "Grace Carter has come over and is staying with her, like a dear," Ruth explained. Later, if Auntie felt better, the girls were to go up to her room.

Ruth, as has appeared, was an extremely impulsive young person. Fortunately, most of her impulses were inspired by a natural kindliness, and a cheerful, youthful energy, with a stratum of good common sense at bottom. There was apt to be method in her madness. Her "plan," for instance, had long been her desire, but before she had never seen the way.

Ruth couldn't wait for the cold boullion to be taken off. "Father, I want to tell them now!" she exclaimed. After his cheerful, "Go ahead, daughter," she burst out: "Barbara, Mollie, won't you go on an automobile tour to Newport with Grace Carter and me, with Aunt Sallie for chaperon? Won't you, can't you come?"

While the amazed girls could only look at her and at each other, she hurried on: "Oh, yes, you probably think I'm crazy. But I'm not. You see it's like this: all my life I have longed to travel by myself; at least, with the people I want, not in a train, or a big crowded boat. Dad knows the feeling; it's what makes him run away from Chicago, and get out on the prairies and ride and ride and ride! I'm a girl, so I can't do that or lots of things. But I can run an automobile. For two years I have just been waiting to get the right crowd. Grace is a dear, but I wanted two more. The other girls I know are all right to meet at dances and to see now and then; but they'd collapse at the thought of starting off on a lark like this. You two—you're different, I knew it the minute I saw you. Besides," she continued, "Grace has been telling me things about you. I always know right off whether I like anybody, and it doesn't take long to find out how much I like them. I like both of you a whole lot—and I know we will have a perfectly delightful trip if you will go with me. If you don't, I simply can't go—that's all. It would be absurd setting off in that great machine with only Grace and Aunt Sallie to rattle around like two peas in a pod. Daddie understands, and he likes you just the way I do—I can see it in his eyes. So it's just up to you! Do you like me a little bit—well, say enough to visit me in my automobile for a month or so? Oh, please say you do!"

She stopped, her voice catching impulsively over the last words. Barbara's eyes were shining. "I don't believe we need to tell you that," she said softly; "you must just know. But there's mother. And we haven't the money."

"Now that's not fair," Ruth broke in. "The money is out of the question altogether. You are my guests. Why, it's you who will do me the favor," she pleaded, as she caught the look of dissent on Barbara's face. "Remember, if you fail me, I can't have my trip at all— and I have been looking forward to it for two whole years. As for your mother, if she will consent to it, Dad and I have a beautiful plan, to keep her and Dad both from being lonely. Poor Dad is sick and tired of hotel cooking and I told him all about your dear little cottage and the dandy tea and cookies your mother makes, and—and—do you suppose your mother would let Dad take his meals with her while we are away? Then he won't be too wretched living all alone up here. Also, you wouldn't have to worry about your mother, nor would I have to worry about Dad. Aunt Sallie has been with him so long that I don't know what he'd do all by himself. He could get on very well, if only your mother would look after him at meals, I know that.

"Now I won't say another word about it for the rest of our lunch. Then we'll run in and call on Aunt Sallie. Afterward we will take the car out and see your mother, and get her to say yes! Then you'll say it, too, won't you? But don't let's spoil this good chicken salad, through worrying about it."

In a more or less complete, yet altogether happy silence, the luncheon was finished. Ruth and her father did not try to force their guests to talk, realizing that the girls would want to think. From the smiling glances the two Stuarts exchanged now and then it was evident they hoped the thinking would have a happy outcome.

After the last course had been served, and the finger bowls, a sprig of rose geranium floating in each, had been pushed aside, Ruth said quietly: "Now we will go to see Aunt Sallie for a few minutes. Daddie, you'll have the machine at the door?"

The girls filed into the elevator, and soon were speeding down a long hall to Aunt Sallie's suite, just across from Ruth's. The latter knocked softly, and Grace Carter came to the door. "Yes, ever so much better," Grace murmured, in reply to Ruth's whispered inquiry. "She wants you to be sure to come in with your friends before they go. Yes; I am sure she would be glad to see them now."

As the girls entered the vestibule of the apartment,

Grace gave Barbara's hand a furtive squeeze, and whispered: "I'll just never recover if you don't come." There was no chance for a reply, for a precise, though rather kindly voice called from the room beyond: "Ruth, please bring your friends in here."

With some trepidation the girls advanced toward "Aunt Sallie." She was a somewhat stout woman, who reclined on a couch in a handsome violet negligée. She scanned the girls sharply for a moment, then in her carefully enunciated syllables, which contrasted oddly with her smooth, plump face, she said: "So you're the young ladies who stop runaway horses! Well, I never could have done it when I was young. But I'm sure I am indebted to you, and I am happy to know you, my dears. I hope and trust, since my madcap niece is bound to take her trip, that you will come along to keep her company."

The girls smiled, and Ruth murmured to them: "You see, you really must come for the sake of my family!" Then Aunt Sallie stretched out two plump, jeweled hands and remarked: "I am sure I shall see a great deal of you very soon, my dears, and you will see all you want to of me. So, if you don't mind, I'll ask you to excuse me now, my head is so tired."

"She likes to take a cat-nap pretty often," explained irreverent Ruth, as soon as they were safely outside the door. "But Aunt Sallie is a good sort, just the same, and the best possible dragon for our trip. Your mother needn't be in the least afraid to trust you to her. Now for your mother," Ruth added as the girls entered the elevator.

In front of the broad piazza the automobile waited on the driveway, with Mr. Stuart as chauffeur. "Pile in," he smiled, and, in a trice, the girls were whirled homeward once more.

There a mighty conference was held. At first, Mrs. Thurston simply gasped. Then she dumbly shook her head. Barbara and Mollie both protested that nothing would persuade them to leave their mother against her wishes. As Ruth said afterwards, "Daddie did the whole thing." He explained to the girls, and to their mother, how brief the separation would be. To the mother he expatiated on the delights and educational value of such a trip. To the girls he hinted, delicately, that perhaps the little mother would get a bit of a rest, all by herself, for a few weeks, even with him to take care of. To all present Mr. Stuart enlarged upon the duty of charity toward him, a homeless vacation visitor, starving from eating only hotel food, and toward his daughter, a sisterless girl with a longing for friends. Though the Thurstons shook their heads, between smiles and tears, at the absurdity of these arguments, they finally said a grateful "yes."

"One really doesn't need any clothes except veils and dusters for an automobile trip, and I have a big extra stock of those," concluded Ruth. "I want to run up here for you people—let me see—to-day is Friday—next Monday morning. That's such a nice day to start."

"Yes," again cried Mollie and Barbara.

The girls joined hands and made a low curtsey to Mrs. Thurston and Mr. Stuart. "Allow me to introduce you," said Ruth in her most impressive voice, "to 'The Automobile Girls' on their way to Newport."

"Long may they flourish!" concluded Mr. Stuart, turning to the girls' mother. "I'll come up with Ruth and help you start them off, Mrs. Thurston. Then, if I may, I will come back and have lunch with you later in the day."

"Till Monday!" called Ruth, and the machine whirled off.

Barbara and Mollie watched it from the gate. "I wish—I wish I could do something for them," mused Barbara, her chin sunk in her hand, her brown eyes showing that soft brightness that only came to them when she was greatly moved.

How well she was to repay the Stuart kith and kin she could not then guess.

CHAPTER IV

Mother's Secret

Mollie danced into the kitchen, waving the feather
duster. "I'm so happy, I can't keep still!" she
declared, waltzing in a circle around her mother and
Barbara, who were in the kitchen washing the breakfast dishes.

"It is just as well you don't have to," Mrs. Thurston
laughed. "But, children, do be sensible a minute," she
urged, as Barbara joined in the dance, still polishing
a breakfast tumbler. "I've been thinking, that going to
Newport, if only to stay a few days, *does* mean more
clothes than automobile coats and motor veils."

"Now, you are not to worry, mother dearest," interrupted Barbara, "or we won't go a single step. Beside,
have you forgotten the twenty-dollar gold-pieces? They
are a fortune, two fortunes really." Barbara had been
doing some pretty deep thinking herself, on the clothes
question, but it would never do to let her thoughts be
known. As elder daughter she tried to save her mother
from all the worries she could. "While there are no men
around in the family, you'll just have to pretend I'm

older son instead of daughter," she used to say. "When Mollie marries I'll resign."

"I'm through dusting," Mollie called from the dining-room. "This time I am surely going to get paper and pencil to put down what clothes we most need, if Barbara won't stop any runaway horses while I am away."

Mollie's golden head and Barbara's tawny one bent anxiously over the paper.

"Ruth's such an impetuous dear! Starting off on our trip Monday does not give us time to get anything new. Mother, will you go in to town shopping for us, and then send the clothes on later? I suppose we shall be on the road some time. Ruth says we are to stop in any of the places we like, and see all the sights along the way," continued Barbara.

Gloves, ribbons, stockings, hair ribbons, and—oh, dear, yes! A pink sash for Bab and a blue one for Mollie. Forty dollars wasn't such a fortune after all. Where was the money left over for the party dresses? Both girls looked a little crestfallen, but Barbara shook her head at Mollie as a signal not to say anything aloud.

Mother had come into the open dining-room door and was watching the girls' faces.

"I've a secret," Mrs. Thurston said, after a minute. "A beautiful secret that I have been keeping to myself for over a year, now. But I think to-day is the best time I can find to tell it." Mrs. Thurston was fragile and blond, like Mollie, with a delicate color in her cheeks, and the sweetest smile in the world.

"It's a nice secret, mother, I can tell by your face." Mollie put her arm around her mother and pulled her down in a chair, while she and Bab sat on either side of her. "Now, out with it!" they both cried.

"Daughters," Mrs. Thurston lowered her voice and spoke in a whisper, "upstairs, in my room in the back part of my desk is an old bank book. What do you think is pressed between the pages?" She paused a minute, and Mollie gave her arm a little shake. "In that book," the mother continued, "are two fifty-dollar bills; one is labeled 'Bab' and the other is labeled 'Baby.'" Mrs. Thurston still called her big, fourteen-year-old daughter "baby" when no one was near.

Mollie and Barbara could only stare at each other, and at their mother in surprise.

"Please, and where did they come from?" queried Barbara.

"They came from nickels and dimes, and sometimes pennies," Mrs. Thurston replied, as pleased and excited as the girls. "Only a week ago, I went to the bank and had the money changed into the two big bills. Oh, I've been saving some time. I saw my girls were growing up, and I imagined that, some day, something nice would happen—not just this, perhaps, but something equally exciting. So I wanted to be ready, and I am. I will get the prettiest clothes I can buy for the money, and I'll have Miss Mattie, the seamstress, in to help me. When you arrive in the fashionable world of Newport, new outfits will be awaiting my two girls."

Mrs. Thurston's face was radiant over the joys in store for her daughters, but Barbara's eyes were full of tears. She knew what pinching and saving, what sacrifices the two banknotes meant.

Soon Bab asked: "You don't need me any more, do you, mother? Because, if you don't, I am going up to look in the treasure chest. I want to find something to re-trim Mollie's hat. The roses are so faded, on the one she is wearing, it will never do to wear with her nice spring suit."

There was a little attic over the cottage, and it almost belonged to Barbara. Up there she used to study her lessons, write poetry, and dream of the wonderful things she hoped to do in order to make mother and Mollie rich.

Barbara skipped over to the trunk, where they kept odds and ends of faded finery, gifts from rich cousins who sent their cast-off clothes to the little girls. "This is like Pandora's chest," laughed Barbara to herself. "It looks as if everything, now, has gone out of it, except Hope."

Bump! bang! crash! the chandelier shivered over Mrs. Thurston and Mollie's heads. Both started up with the one word, "Bab," on their lips. It was impossible to know what she would attempt, or what would happen to her next.

Just as they reached the foot of the attic steps an apologetic head appeared over the railing. "I am not hurt," Bab's voice explained. "I just tried to move the old bureau so I could see better, and I knocked over a trunk. I am so sorry, mother, but the trunk has broken open. It is that old one of yours. I know it made an awful racket!"

"It does not matter, child," Mrs. Thurston said in a relieved tone, when she saw what had actually happened. "Nothing matters, since you have not killed yourself."

She bent over her trunk. The old lock had been loosened by the fall, and the top had tumbled off. On the floor were a yellow roll of papers, and a quaint carved fan. Mrs. Thurston picked them up. The papers she dropped in the tray of the trunk, but the fan she kept in her hand. "This little fan," she said, "I used at the last party your father and I attended together the week before we were married. I have kept it a long time, and I think it very beautiful." She opened, with loving fingers, a fan of delicately-carved ivory, mounted in silver, and hung on a curious silver chain. "Your great-uncle brought it to me from China, when I was just your age, Mollie! It was given him by a viceroy, in recognition of a service rendered. Which of my daughters would like to take this fan to Newport?"

Barbara shook her head, while Mollie looked at it with longing eyes. "I don't believe either of us had better take it," protested Bab, "you have kept it so carefully all this time."

But her mother said decidedly: "I saved it only for

you girls. Here, Mollie, suppose you take it; we will find something else for Bab."

As Mollie and her mother lifted out the tray of the old trunk, Bab's eyes caught sight of the roll of papers, and she picked them up.

"Hello, hello!" a cheerful voice sounded from downstairs.

"It's Grace Carter," said Mollie. "You don't mind her coming up, do you, mother?"

Grace was almost a third daughter at the little Thurston cottage. Her own home was big and dull! her mother was a stern, cold woman, and her two brothers were much older than Grace.

"No," said Mrs. Thurston, going on with her search.

"I couldn't keep away, chilluns," apologized Grace as she came upstairs. "Mother told me I'd be dreadfully in the way, but I just had to talk about our trip. Isn't it too splendid! You are not having secrets, are you?"

"Not from you," Mrs. Thurston said. "See what I have found for Bab." Mrs. Thurston held out an open jewel-case. In it was a beautiful spray of pink coral, and a round coral pin.

"I think, Bab, dear," she said, "you are old enough, now, for such simple jewelry. I will buy you a white muslin, and you can wear this pin at your throat and the spray in your hair. Then, with a coral ribbon sash, who knows but you may be one of the belles of a Newport party?"

Barbara flushed with pleasure over the gifts, but she looked so embarrassed at her mother's compliment that Mollie and Grace both laughed.

"I declare," Grace said, "you have less vanity than any girl in the world. Oh, wasn't it fortunate I discovered your money yesterday? Just as we all jumped out of the car I heard something clink, and picked up one of your twenty dollars. Harry Townsend said he found the other tucked away in the leather of the front seat."

"And I sat in the back seat all the time I was in the car," reflected Barbara, under her breath.

When a turquoise blue heart on a string of tiny beads had been added to Mollie's "going-away" treasures, she and Grace went down stairs.

Barbara still held the roll of papers in her hand and kept turning them over and over, trying to read the faded writing. She caught sight of her father's signature. "Are these papers valuable?" she asked her mother.

Mrs. Thurston sighed deeply as she answered: "They are old papers of your father's. Put them away again. I never like to look at them. I found them in his business suit after he was dead. He had sent it to the tailor, and had forgotten all about it." Mrs. Thurston took the papers from Barbara's hand and put them back into her trunk.

"Do you think they are valuable, mother?" persisted Barbara.

"I don't think so," her mother concluded. "Your

uncle told me he looked over all your father's papers that were of any value."

After the two had mended the lock of the old trunk, and turned to leave the attic, Barbara was still thinking. "Dearest," she said thoughtfully, "would you mind my going through those papers some time?" To herself Bab added: "I'd like to ask a clever business man, like Mr. Stuart, to explain them to me."

But Mrs. Thurston sighed as she said: "Oh, yes, you may look them over, some day, if you like. It won't make any difference."

What difference it might make neither Mrs. Thurston or Barbara could then know.

CHAPTER V

The Glorious Start

Before daylight, on the great day, Mollie's two arms encircled a sleepy Barbara, and a soft voice whispered in her ear: "It isn't true, is it, Bab, that you and I, two insignificant little girls, who never could have conceived of anything so glorious, are off to-day for Newport, escorted by Ruth's distinguished friend, 'Mr. A. Bubble'?"

Barbara was wide awake in a minute.

"I suppose it's true," she said, "because it was last night, before we went to bed. Otherwise I would think we had both dreamed it."

The two girls talked in excited whispers. It wouldn't do to waken mother any earlier than they must, for she was tired with their preparations, though her daughters had persuaded her to have a little country girl in to help with the work, now that she was to have so important a person as Mr. Stuart for "boarder."

But at seven o'clock it was mother who called:

"Get up, girls. It is time for coffee and clothes, if you are to start off at ten as you promised. It will not do

to keep Miss Stuart and the girls waiting. As for Mr.
A. Bubble, I don't believe he can stand still, even if he
tries."

Aunt Sallie having called on Sunday afternoon, had
waived ceremony and stayed to tea in the tiny cottage, so
impressed was she with Mrs. Thurston's quiet charm
and gentle manners.

The two girls hurried into their kimonos. Mother
had suggested these garments for this morning, since
they were to dress so soon afterwards in their "going
away" clothes.

By the time that Barbara and Mollie had put on
their pretty brown and blue serge suits, with their dust
coats over them, they heard strange noises on the front
porch, mingled with giggles and whispers. Barbara was
putting the sixth hat pin into her hat, and tying the
motor veil so tightly under her chin that it choked her,
when Mollie peeped out the front window.

"It's a surprise party, I do believe," she whispered.
"There's Harold Smith, with a big bunch of pink roses.
I know they are for you. The girls have little bundles
in their hands. What fun! I didn't know they had
heard of our trip. How fast news does fly around this
village."

While Mollie and Barbara were saying their good-
byes on their little veranda there was equal excitement
at the big hotel.

Before breakfast Ruth had gone out to the garage
with her arm in her father's.

"I want to see with my own eyes, Dad," she said, "that the machine is all right. Isn't it well that I have a taste for mechanics, even though I am a girl? Suppose I hadn't studied all those automobile books with you until I could say them backwards, and hadn't helped you over all the accidents—you never would have let me go on this heavenly trip, would you? I am going to be as careful as can be, just to show you did right to trust me, also not to give Aunt Sallie a chance to say, 'I told you so.'"

Ruth had pretty, sunny, red-gold hair and big, gray-blue eyes. Though she wasn't exactly a beauty, her face was so frank, and her coloring so fresh and lovely, many people thought her very good-looking.

Mr. Stuart smiled at his daughter's enthusiasm. "She's 'a chip of the old block,'" he said to himself. "She loves fun and adventure and 'getting there,' like a man. I am not going to stand in her way."

Mr. Stuart was feeling rather nervous about the trip this morning, but he didn't intend Ruth to know.

To judge by the looks of the automobile, the chauffeur must have been up all night. The machinery was cleaned and oiled. The extra tires, in their dark red leather cases, were strapped to the sides of the car. A great box of extra rugs and wraps, rubber covers for the machine and mackintoshes in case of rain, was tied on the back. Between the seats was an open hamper for lunch, with an English tea service in one compartment, and cups, saucers, a teapot and a hot-water jug and alcohol lamp, all complete. The luncheon was to be sent down later from the hotel.

"You are to take your meals at the inns along the way, when you prefer," Mr. Stuart had explained, "but I don't mean to have you run the risk of starving in case you are delayed, or an accident occurs. Be sure to take your picnic lunch along with you, when you start out each day. What you don't eat, feed to the small boys along the road, who will insist on playing guide."

Aunt Sallie was the only one of the hotel party who enjoyed breakfast. Grace had driven over early, and was breakfasting with Ruth in order to save delay. Both the girls and Mr. Stuart were too excited to take much interest in their bacon and eggs, but Aunt Sallie ate with a resigned expression that seemed to say: "Perhaps this is my last meal on earth." Yet, secretly, she was almost as delighted as were the girls in the prospect of the trip.

"Now, Sallie, you are not to go if you don't wish to," Mr. Stuart had protested. "You must not let Ruth drag you into this trip against your will."

But all he could persuade his sister to answer was: "If Ruth is going on such an extraordinary excursion, then, at least, I shall be along to see that nothing worse happens to her."

Gladys Le Baron came into the dining-room, stopping in front of Ruth's table. "You dear things," she drawled in her most careful society manner, "how can you look so fresh so early in the morning? I hope you appreciate my getting up to see you off." Gladys wore a lingerie frock more appropriate for a party than for the breakfast room.

But Ruth answered good naturedly. "I do appreciate it, if it is such an effort for you. Did you know Mr. Townsend is going to ride over to the Thurston's with us to see us start? He tells me you and he are both to be in Newport while we are there."

"Yes," Gladys declared with more airs than before. "Mrs. Erwin has asked me to be one of the house-party she's to have for her ball. She told me I could bring a friend along, and I have asked Mr. Townsend."

"Wonderful! We won't expect you to associate with us!" laughed Grace.

"Gladys," Ruth asked, "would you like to drive over to Mrs. Thurston's with us? Father is going, and the carriage will be there to bring him back."

"I would like to go," murmured Gladys, "if I didn't have on this old frock. I don't know Mollie and Barbara very well, but I suppose I shall have to see a great deal of them, now you have taken them up. I wonder how they will behave at Newport? They have hardly been out of Kingsbridge before."

Grace and Ruth both looked angry, and Mr. Stuart broke in, quite curtly: "I am sure we can depend on their behaving becomingly, which is all that is necessary at Newport or any other place." Ruth's father was a business acquaintance of Gladys's father, and had known her mother when the latter was a girl, but the airs of Mrs. Le Baron and her society daughter were too much for his western common sense. Only Aunt Sallie was impressed by their imposing manner.

Ruth was very popular at the big summer hotel, and a number of the guests had assembled to see her off. But Ruth let her father run the car and sat quietly by his side. "You'll turn over the command to me, captain, won't you, when the trip really commences?" and she squeezed his arm with a little movement of affection.

"Yes, lieutenant," Mr. Stuart said quietly.

"Oh, Miss Ruth," called Mr. Townsend from the back seat, "do show all these people how you can handle your car!" But she only shook her head.

"Goodness me, what are all those people doing on Mrs. Thurston's porch?" Ruth asked, in alarm. "I hope nothing has happened." But, as the car neared the quiet little house, which stood midway between the hotel and the New York high road, she saw the party of young people gathered on the front lawn.

"It's only their friends, come to say good-bye to them," Harry volunteered. In answer to "What a bore!" from Gladys, he continued: "I don't know why you should think it a bore. Miss Stuart enjoys her friends's popularity." Mr. Townsend had been trying, for several weeks, to make himself equally agreeable to Ruth and Gladys. They were both very wealthy, and it seemed wise to him to associate with rich people. But as Ruth was not easily impressed with what she called "just foolishness," he had become very intimate with Gladys Le Baron.

When Mr. Stuart tooted the horn to announce their approach to the cottage a chorus of tin horns answered him from Mrs. Thurston's front garden. As the car drew up to the gate, the boys and girls began to sing, "See the Conquering Hero Comes," while Barbara ran down to the car and Mollie urged her friends to be quieter. "I just don't know what Miss Stuart and Mr. Stuart will think of us!" she blushingly remonstrated.

But Aunt Sallie and Mr. Stuart were in for all the fun going this morning. Barbara was invited to call her seven friends who had come to give the girls a send-off, down to meet the occupants of the car. Even Gladys, as she was forced to get out of the automobile to let the other travelers in, was condescending enough to permit Harold Smith to assist her. Harold was an old friend of Barbara's, and one of the cleverest boys in the village.

Mr. Stuart went into the house for the suit cases and satchels, which were all the girls were to take with them, as they were to manage with as few clothes as possible. It had been arranged that extra luggage was to be expressed to them along the way.

Barbara had caught Mollie storing away a sample package of cold cream among her most treasured possessions.

"I am sure I don't see why you should laugh so," Mollie urged quite seriously. "It reads on the label 'especially adapted for automobile travelers to remove dust and tan from the face after the drive.' Aren't we going to be automobile travelers?"

"Sure and we a'ire," said Bab, imitating the old Irish washerwoman, "and it shall put grease on its nose if it likes."

"Come, daughter," said Mr. Stuart finally, as Ruth was trying to explain to a group of admiring boys the first principles of running an automobile. She talked as familiarly of an emergency brake and a steering wheel, of horse power and speed-transmission, as most girls talk of frills and furbelows.

"It's ten-thirty," Mr. Stuart continued, "and, if this party is to be a strictly on time affair, you must be off! You couldn't have a more wonderful day."

It was late in the month of June. The summer clouds were sailing overhead, great bubbles of white foam thrown up into the blue depth of the sky. The sun shone brightly and the whole atmosphere was perfumed with the bloom of the honeysuckle, that hung in yellow clusters from Mrs. Thurston's porch.

Barbara and Mollie flung their arms around their mother until she was completely enveloped in their embrace. Ruth kissed her father, and put her hand to her trim leather cap with a military salute. "It's all right, captain," she said; "I'll bring my crew and good ship 'Bubble' safely into port."

Aunt Sallie was anxious to be off. She could see that Mrs. Thurston was on the verge of tears at the thought of parting with her daughters. Still the young people were laughing and talking, and storing their little gifts under the seats in the car, as though they had all day before them.

"Hurry, child," Aunt Sallie urged, reaching out a hand to Mollie. "Jump up on the back seat with Grace and me. We will let Mistress Barbara sit with Ruth for the first of the journey." Aunt Sallie was very imposing in a violet silk traveling coat, with a veil and hat of the same shade; indeed, Miss Sallie had a fancy for a "touch of lavender" in everything she wore. With her snow-white hair, and commanding appearance, she would add prestige to the party, Mollie thought, no matter how dusty and wind-blown the rest of them might appear.

The girls hopped gayly in. Toot, toot, toot! the horn blew three times. Chug-chug-chug! and the great machine began to breathe with deep, muffled roars. Mr. Stuart gave the starting crank a strong turn, and the car slid gracefully along the road, red, blue, pink and violet motor veils floating behind in the breeze.

"Here's good luck to you!" shouted Harold Smith, and roses and flowers of every kind were flung after them. Mollie and Grace picked up those that fell into their laps, and turned to wave their hands and throw kisses for good-bye.

"They look like a rainbow," said Mr. Stuart, turning to Mrs. Thurston, who was no longer trying to hide her tears. Then he smiled at her gently. She was such a tiny, girlish-looking little woman, it was hard to think of her as the mother of two nearly grown-up daughters. "I expect," he continued, "that that rainbow holds most of our promise of sunshine."

They were still watching the car!

Down to the gate, at the furthest end of the road, a baby boy, chubby and fat, had crawled on two round, turned-in legs. There was something unusual going on down the street. He could hear strange noises, but, though he stuck his small nose through the fence, he was still unable to see. Just as Ruth's car was almost in front of the house, open flew the stubborn old gate, and the child flung himself out in the middle of the road, just in front of the wonderful red thing he could see flying toward him. The baby was too young to understand the danger.

From the watchers at Mrs. Thurston's came a cry of horror. A thrill of terror passed through the occupants of the car. Ruth's face turned white. Like a flash, she slowed a little, turned her steering wheel and with a wide sweep drove her motor to the far side of the road, then straight on out of the path of the wondering baby.

Mr. Stuart's, "Bravo, daughter!" was lost in his throat. But the little group of waiting friends gave three cheers for the girl chauffeur, which Ruth heard even at such a distance. Truly "The Automobile Girls" were fairly started on their adventures.

CHAPTER VI

. . . .

What Happened the First Day

The car flew along by sunny meadows and farms. New York was the first day's goal.

"Barbara," Ruth said to her next-door neighbor, "you are hereby appointed royal geographer and guide-extraordinary to this party! Here is the route-book. It will be up to you to show us which roads we are to take. It is a pretty hard job, as I well know from experience; but then, honors come hard. You don't need to worry to-day. I know this coast trip into New York as well as I know my A.B.C.'s. I have often come along this way with father. Let's have a perfectly beautiful time in New York. We'll make Aunt Sallie chaperon us while we do the town, or, at least, a part of it. Have you ever been to a roof garden?"

Barbara's eyes danced. It didn't sound quite right somehow—a roof garden—but then they were out for experiences, and Miss Sallie wouldn't let them do anything really wrong.

Ruth glanced out of the corner of her eye at Barbara. Miss Stuart was a good little chauffeur who never allowed her attention to be distracted from running her car, no matter what was being talked of around her, nor how much she was interested, but she couldn't help laughing at Barbara's expression; it told so plainly all that was going on inside her head.

"I do assure you, Miss Barbara Thurston, that a roof garden may be a fairly respectable thing, quite well suited to entertaining, without shocking either Miss Sallie Stuart or her four charming protégées." Ruth called back: "Aunt Sallie, will you take us up on the Waldorf roof to-night? You know we are going to stay at the Waldorf Hotel, girls. Father said we might enjoy the experience, and it would be all right with Aunt Sallie for chaperon."

Grace pinched Mollie's arm to express her rapture, and that little maiden simply gasped with delight. It was Mollie, not Barbara, of the two sisters, who had the greatest yearning for wealth and society, and the beautiful clothes and wonderful people that she believed went along with it. Barbara was an out-door girl, who loved tennis and all the sports, and could swim like a fish. An artist who spent his summers at Kingsbridge, once called her a brown sea-gull, when he saw her lithe brown body dart off the great pier to dive deep into the water.

Aunt Sallie had been taking a brief cat-nap, before Ruth's question, and awakened in high good humor. "Why, yes, children," she answered, "it will be very pleasant to go up on the roof to-night, after we have had our baths and our dinners. I am quite disposed to let you do just what you like, so long as you behave yourselves."

Grace Carter pressed Aunt Sallie's fat hand, as a message of thanks. Grace was Aunt Sallie's favorite among Ruth's friends. "She is a quiet, lady-like girl, who does not do unexpected things that get on one's nerves," Miss Sallie had once explained to Ruth. "Now, Aunt Sallie," Ruth had protested, "I know I *do* get on your nerves sometimes, but you know you need me to stir you up. Think how dull you would be without me!" And Aunt Sallie had answered, with unexpected feeling: "I would be very dull, indeed, my dear."

The girls were full of their plans for the evening.

"That is why Ruth told us each to put a muslin dress in our suit cases! Ruth, are you going to think up a fresh surprise every day? It's just too splendid!" Mollie spoke in a tone of such fervent emotion that everyone in the car laughed.

"I don't suppose I can manage a surprise every day, Molliekins," Ruth called back over her shoulder, "but I mean to think up as many as I possibly can. We are going to have the time of our lives, you know, and something must happen to make it."

All this time the car had been flying faster than the girls could talk. "This is 'going some,'" commented Ruth, laughing.

When they came into Lakewood Ruth slowed up, as she had promised her father not to go any faster than the law allowed. "I cross my heart and body, Dad," she had said. "Think of four lovely maidens and their handsome duenna languishing in jail instead of flying along the road to Newport. Honest Injun! father, I'll read every automobile sign from here to Jehosaphat, if we ever decide to travel that way."

In Lakewood, Ruth drove her car around the wonderful pine shaded lake.

"It's a winter resort," she explained to her companions. "Nearly all the cottages and hotels are closed in the summer, but I wanted you to have a smell of the pines. It will give you strength for the rest of the trip."

Silence fell on the party as they skimmed out of Lakewood. After so much excitement it was pleasant to look at things without having to talk.

Mollie had begun, once in a while, to tap the lunch basket with her foot. The fresh air and the long ride had made her desperately hungry. She really couldn't remember having eaten any breakfast in the excitement of getting off. But nobody said f-o-o-d! She felt she was the youngest member of the party and should not make suggestions before Miss Sallie.

Ruth turned into a narrow lane; a sign post pointed the way to a deserted village.

"Oh, dear me!" sighed Mollie to herself. "Why are we going to a deserted village, just as we are dying of hunger!"

Ruth said never a word. She passed some tumbledown old cottages of a century ago, then an old iron foundry, and drew up with a great flourish before an old stone house, green with moss and ivy and fragrant with a "lovely" odor of cooking! There were little tables set out on the lawn and on the old-fashioned veranda, and soon the party was reveling in lunch.

"I didn't know food could be so heavenly," whispered Mollie in Bab's ear, when they were back in the car, for Grace had begged for a seat by the chauffeur for the afternoon trip.

Soon Ruth left the country behind, and came out on the sea-coast road that ran through Long Branch, Deal Beach, Monmouth and Seabright.

From carriages and other automobiles, and along the promenades, everyone smiled at the crimson car full of happy, laughing girls.

Ruth was driving in her best fashion, making all the speed she could, with the thought of town fifty miles or more ahead. "It is a sight to see," quoth Barbara, "the way the fairy princess handles her chariot of fire."

It was a little after four o'clock when the car boarded the Staten Island ferry and finally crossed to the New York shore.

"You see, Bab," Mollie said, trying to stuff her curls under her motor cap and to rub the dust from her rosy cheeks with a tiny pocket handkerchief as they sped up Broadway, "I might be dreadfully embarrassed arriving at the Waldorf looking the way I do, if I were not in a motor car, but riding in an automobile makes one feel so awfully swell that nothing matters. Isn't it lovely just to feel important for once? You know it is, Bab, and you needn't say no! It's silly to pretend."

Miss Sallie was again on the border of slumberland, so that Mollie and Barbara could have their low-voiced talk.

"Does Ruth know I have never even been to New York before?" asked Mollie. "I hope I won't seem very green about things. You must tell me if I do, Bab."

But Bab only laughed and shook her head. "You are a foolish baby," she said.

Two respectful porters at the Waldorf helped a dusty, crumpled party out of the big red touring car.

The girls, a little dazed, followed Miss Sallie through a maze of palms and servants in livery, with handsomely dressed people strolling through the halls, until their suite of rooms, which Mr. Stuart had engaged by telegraph a few days before, was reached.

The three rooms adjoined, only separated by white tile bathrooms. Miss Sallie, naturally, had a room to herself, and it was decided that Ruth and Grace were to sleep together, leaving the sisters to themselves.

"Isn't it too beautiful!" sighed Mollie, standing in the midst of their luxurious chamber, gazing around at the single brass beds, with their rose-colored draperies, and the ivory-striped satin wall paper, garlanded in pink flowers. Ruth and Grace were equally fine in a room decorated in blue, and, even in the Waldorf, Miss Sallie's taste seemed to have been consulted, as her room was in her favorite violet shade.

In some mysterious way the crumpled muslin dresses were taken downstairs by a maid, and came back smooth and fresh. Even Miss Sallie's elaborate chiffon gown looked as though it had just come home from the modiste's.

"O Ruth! Ruth!" Mollie exclaimed, as the four girls made their way to the dining-room, Miss Sallie in the lead, "I didn't know there could be such a magnificent place in the world as this. I don't know what I can ever do to repay you, except to love you and be grateful my whole life long."

"Well, I am sure that is all the gratitude I should ever want, Mollie," laughed Ruth. "But wait until you see the houses at Newport."

All eyes near the door turned to see the little automobile party enter the "palm room." Miss Sallie swept ahead in her black lace and chiffon, looking very handsome and impressive. Barbara and Grace came next; Barbara with her red-brown hair breaking into willful curves and waves, her big brown eyes glowing with pleasure, and the deep red showing in her olive cheeks; Grace with her look of refinement and gentle dignity. The blond maidens came in last. Ruth's bright gold hair and fresh coloring showed to best advantage in a dainty white muslin and lace frock. She was half a head taller than dainty Mollie, who looked like a flower with her yellow curls gathered in a soft cluster at the back of her neck and tied with a black velvet ribbon.

On the Waldorf roof, Miss Stuart and the girls sat

under an orange tree, hung in some mysterious way with golden oranges. The whole place was decorated with palms and evergreens and beautiful flowers. The soft, shaded yellow lights rivaled the moonlight that glowed above.

"It's like the enchanted garden in the French fairy story, isn't it, Miss Sallie? Where the flowers and fruits bloomed all the year round?" whispered Barbara, who sat next their chaperon.

Miss Sallie smiled very kindly at her enthusiasm.

"I expect it is, but I am afraid I have forgotten the story. It has been a long time, remember, Barbara, since fairies and I have had much to say to each other."

Barbara blushed. "Oh, I am not so young as all that, Miss Sallie; but I have never forgotten the fairy tales I read when I was a little girl. Though I must confess I liked boys' stories better. I just love adventures!" And Barbara's eyes shone. In a little while the music commenced, and she forgot everything but that.

Mollie was differently occupied. What she liked best was to gaze around her at the women in their jewels and wonderful gowns.

Just across from her on the other side of the aisle was a rarely beautiful woman in a white lace gown, with a string of pearls round her throat, and a pearl and diamond butterfly that glowed and sparkled in her hair.

Mollie was so fascinated by her beauty that she couldn't help watching this stranger, and even overhearing a little of her conversation. "It isn't exactly eaves-dropping," Mollie apologized to herself, "because I don't know them and they can never possibly know me." So nobody noticed, but Mollie, that when the woman gave a laughing toss of her head in answer to some question from her husband, who sat back of her, that the beautiful, jeweled butterfly slipped softly out of her hair, fell into the softer lace folds of her gown and then down—down—to the floor!

The little girl waited half a minute. No one else had noticed the loss. At any time an usher might come down the aisle and crush the exquisite jewel. Mollie forgot herself and her shyness. If it had been Barbara she would not have minded, but Mollie was timid before strangers. She slipped quietly across the aisle and picked up the butterfly.

"I beg your pardon," her soft voice explained, "but I saw this fall from your hair, and, as you did not notice it, I was afraid it might be crushed."

The lovely woman turned in surprise. It is just as well to call her "the lovely lady," now, for that was Mollie's name for her ever afterwards.

"My dear," she said, "I am very grateful to you. How could I have failed to see it? I am especially obliged to you, because I am very fond of this ornament."

Mollie blushed rosy-red, as the people close to them had observed what had happened and were watching her. As she tried to slip over to her seat, the lady reached out and gave the child's hand a gentle squeeze of thanks, glancing across as she did so to see what friends the little girl was with, and so caught Ruth Stuart's eye.

The intermission came at this minute.

"Why, Ruth Stuart!" Mollie, to her surprise, heard her friend's name called in a low voice, and Ruth came across to them.

"It's Mrs. Cartwright," she said. "I am so pleased! I didn't suppose you would remember me."

"Of course I remember you, Ruth," Mrs. Cartwright protested. "It has been only two years since I saw you at my own wedding in Chicago. My memory is surely longer than that. Isn't that your aunt, Miss Stuart?" Mrs. Cartwright moved across the aisle to speak to Miss Sallie and to introduce her husband. When they had shaken hands, Mrs. Cartwright asked: "May I know what you are doing in this part of the world at this season?"

"I am playing chaperon to my madcap niece and her three friends, who are doing an automobile trip to Newport without a man. Ruth is her own chauffeur," Miss Sallie explained, laughing.

"How jolly of you, Ruth, and how clever! I am so glad you are going to Newport. Did you know my summer place is down there? I am only in town for a day or two. My husband had to come on business and I am with him. We shall be motoring home, soon, and may pass you if you are to take things slowly. Why not join me at New Haven? My husband's brother is a junior at Yale, and we've promised to stop there for a day. There is a dance on at Alumni Hall. I'd be too popular for words if I could take you four pretty girls along with me!"

Ruth turned to her aunt with glowing eyes. "We did want to see the college dreadfully," she said. "I have never seen a big Eastern university. We didn't dream of knowing anybody who would show us around. Wouldn't it be too much for you to have us all on your hands?"

"Certainly not," said Mrs. Cartwright, "but a most decided pleasure. I shall meet you in New Haven, say, day after to-morrow, and I'll telegraph to-night to my brother, whose name is Donald Cartwright, by the way, to expect us."

The music was about to begin again, but, before Mrs. Cartwright went over to her seat, she put her hand on Mollie's curls. "I must see this little girl often at Newport. Then I can thank her better for saving my lovely butterfly for me. I hope to make all of you have a beautiful time." She put the jewel into her hair again, and Mollie looked at it thoughtfully. She was to know it again some day, under stranger circumstances.

CHAPTER VII

Showing Their Mettle

"Girls!" Aunt Sallie said solemnly next morning, as Mr. Cartwright and two footmen helped her into the motor car, while Barbara, Grace and Mollie stood around holding her extra veils, her magazines and pocketbook. "I feel, in my bones, that it is going to rain to-day. I think we had better stay in town."

"Oh, Aunt Sallie!" Ruth's hand was already on the spark of her steering wheel, and she was bouncing up and down on her seat in her impatience to be off. "It's simply a splendid day! Look at the sun!" She leaned over to Mr. Cartwright. "Do say something to cheer Aunt Sallie up. If she loses her nerve now, we'll never have our trip."

Mr. and Mrs. Cartwright both reassured her. "The paper says clear weather and light winds, Miss Stuart. You'll have a beautiful day of it. Remember we shall meet you in New Haven to-morrow, and you have promised to wait for us."

Aunt Sallie settled herself resignedly into her violet cushions, holding her smelling bottle to her nose. "Very well, young people, have it your own way," she relented. "But, mark my words, it will rain before night. I have a shoulderblade that is a better weather prophet than all your bureaus."

"You're much too handsome a woman," laughed Ruth, the other girls joining her, "to talk like Katisha, in the 'Mikado,' who had the famous shoulderblade that people came miles to see."

Ruth was steering her car through Fifth Avenue, so Aunt Sallie merely smiled at her own expense, adding: "You're a very disrespectful niece, Ruth."

"I'd get on my knees to apologize, Auntie," declared Ruth, "only there isn't room, and we'd certainly be run into, if I did."

Barbara was poring over the route book. Her duty as guide to the automobile party really began to-day, and she was studying every inch of the road map. What would she do if they were lost?

"You may look up from that book just once in every fifteen minutes, Guide Thurston," Ruth said, pretending to be serious over Barbara's worried look. "We promise not to eat you if you do get us a little out of our way. The roads are well posted. What shall we do if we meet some bandits?"

"Leave them to me," boasted Barbara. "I suppose it's my fate to play man of the party."

"And what of the chauffeur?" Ruth protested. "I wonder what any of us could do if we got into danger."

The day was apparently lovely. The girls were in the wildest spirits.

"I never believed until this minute," announced Mollie, "that we were actually going on the trip to Newport. I felt every moment something would happen to stop us. I even dreamed, last night, that we met a great giant in the road, and he roared at us, 'I never allow red motor cars with brass trimmings to pass along this road!' Ruth wouldn't pay the least attention to him, but kept straight ahead, until he picked up the car and started to pitch us over in a ditch. Then Ruth cried: 'Hold on there! If you won't let a red car pass, I'll go back to town and have mine painted green. I must have my trip.' Just as she turned around and started back, I woke up. Wasn't it awful?"

"You are a goose," said Grace, rather nervously. "It isn't a sign of anything, is it? You ought not to tell your dreams after breakfast. You may make them come true."

Barbara and Ruth both shouted with laughter, for Mollie answered just as seriously: "You're wrong, Grace; it's telling dreams before breakfast that makes them come true. I was particularly careful to wait."

The car passed swiftly through the town in the early morning. Soon the spires and towers of the city were no longer visible.

"Hurrah for the Boston Post Road!" sang Barbara, as the car swung into the famous old highway.

"And hurrah for Barbara for discovering it!" teased Ruth. "Now, clear the track, fellow autoists and slow coach drivers! We know where we're going, and we're on the way!"

It had been decided to make a straight trip through to New Haven, and to wait there for Mrs. Cartwright. Miss Sallie had insisted on some rest, and the girls were wild to see the college—and the college men.

"It will be sure enough sport," Ruth confided, "to have one dance with all the partners needed to go round." Men were as scarce at the Kingsbridge Hotel as they were in other summer resorts, and Ruth was tired of Harry Townsend and his kind, who liked to stay around the hotel, making eyes at all the girls they saw.

"Yes," said Barbara thoughtfully, "it will be fun. Yet, Ruth, suppose we are sticks and no one dances with us?" Barbara didn't like the thought of being a wallflower. Ruth laughed and quickly replied, "Oh, Mrs. Cartwright is awfully jolly and popular, so we will have plenty of invitations to dance."

"Ruth," said Miss Sallie, a little after noon, when they had passed, without a hitch, through a number of beautiful Connecticut towns, and were speeding along an open road, with a view of the waters of Long Island Sound to the right of them, "I have not looked at my watch lately, but I've an impression I am hungry. As long as we have made up our minds to eat the luncheon

Miss Sallie laughed. "There are some people at Newport who are not summer people," she explained. "You must remember that it is an old New England town, and there are thousands of people who live there the year around. My brother has persuaded some old friends of ours, who used to be very wealthy when I was a girl, to take us to board with them. There are very few hotels."

Several times during their talk Ruth's eyes had wandered a little anxiously to the sky above them. Every now and then the shadows darkened under the old elm where they were eating their luncheon, bringing a sudden coolness to the summer atmosphere.

"Aunt Sallie made me nervous about the weather with that story of her shoulderblade," Ruth argued with herself. So she was the first to say: "Come, we had better be off. What a lot of time we've wasted!"

"No hurry, Ruth," Aunt Sallie answered, placidly. "New Haven is no great distance. We shall be there before dark."

It was fully half after two before the automobile girls had gathered up their belongings and were again comfortably disposed in the car.

"It certainly is great, Ruth, the way you crank up your own car," Grace declared. "It must take an awful lot of strength, doesn't it?"

"Yes," admitted Ruth, as she jumped back into her automobile and the car plunged on ahead. "But I've a strong right arm. I don't row and play tennis for noth-

the hotel has put up for us, why not stop along the road here, and have a picnic?"

"Good for you, Aunt Sallie!" said Grace, emphatically. "This is a beauty place. Ruth can leave the car right here, and we can go up under that elm and make tea. What larks!"

The girls all piled out, carrying the big lunch hamper between them. On the stump of an old tree the alcohol lamp was set up and tea was quickly brewed. Then the girls formed a circle on the ground, while Miss Sallie, from her throne of violet silk pillows, gave directions about setting the lunch table.

No one noticed how the time passed. No one could notice, all were having such a jolly time; even Miss Sallie was now in excellent spirits. She had been in Newport several times before, and the girls were full of questions.

Mollie leaned her head against Miss Sallie's knee, so intimate had she grown in a day and a half with that awe-inspiring person. "Is it true," she inquired in a voice of reverence, "that every person who lives in Newport is a millionaire?"

"And are the streets paved with gold, Miss Sallie?" queried Grace. She was Mollie's special friend, and fond of teasing her. "I read that the water at Bailey's Beach is perfumed every morning before the ladies go in bathing, and that all the fish that come from near there taste like cologne."

ing. Father says it takes skill and courage, as well as strength, to drive a car. I hope I'm not boasting; it's only that father believes girls should attempt to do things as well as boys. Girls could do a lot more if they tried harder. 'Sometimes,' Dad says, 'gumption counts for more than brute force.'"

"Whew, Ruth! You talk like a suffragette," objected Grace.

"Well, maybe I am one," said Ruth. "I'm from the West, where they raise strong-minded women. What do you say, Barbara?"

"I don't know," replied Barbara. "I would not like to go to war, and I'm awfully afraid I'd run from a burglar in the dark."

"Who'd have thought Barbara would confess to being a coward?" Grace broke in, just to see what Bab would say. But Bab wouldn't answer. "I don't know what I would do," she ended.

"Anyhow," said Miss Ruth, from her position of dignity on the chauffeur's seat, "I should be allowed to vote on laws for motor cars, as long as I can run a machine without a man."

"My dear Ruth," interposed Miss Sallie at last, "I beg of you, don't vote in my lifetime. Girls, in my day, would never have dreamed of such a thing."

"Oh, well, Auntie," answered Ruth, "I wouldn't worry about it now. Who knows when I may have a chance to vote?"

Ruth was worried by the clouds overhead, so she

ran her machine at full speed. It took some time and
ingenuity to make their way through Bridgeport, a big,
bustling town with crowded streets. By this time the
clouds had lifted, and, for the next hour, Ruth forgot
the rain. She and Barbara were having a serious talk
on the front seat. Mollie and Grace, with their arms
around each other, were almost as quiet as Aunt Sallie;
indeed, they were more so, for that good soul was gently
snoring.

"If we should have any adventures, Bab," said Ruth,
"I wonder if we'd be equal to them? I'll wager you would
be. Father says that when people are not too sure of
themselves before a thing happens, they are likely to be
brave at the critical minute."

The car was going down a hill with a steep incline.
Ruth's hand was on the brake. Biff! Biff! Bang! Bang!
A cannon ball seemed to have exploded under them.
Miss Sallie sat up very straight, with an expression
of great dignity; Grace and Mollie gave little screams,
and Barbara looked as though she were willing to be
defended if anything very dreadful had happened.

Only Ruth dared laugh. "You're not killed, girls,"
she said. "You might as well get used to that racket; it
happens to the best regulated motor cars. It is only a
bursted tire; but it might have been kind enough to have
happened in town, instead of on this deserted country
road. Oh, dear me!" she next ejaculated, for, before she
could stop her car, it had skidded, and the front wheel
was imbedded in a deep hole in the road.

"Get out, please," Ruth ordered. "Grace, will you find a stone for me? I must try to brace this wheel. Did I say something about skill, instead of strength, and not needing a man?" Ruth had taken off her coat and rolled up her sleeves in a business-like fashion.

"I have helped father with a punctured tire before." She tugged at the old tire, which hung limp and useless by this time. She was talking very cheerfully, though Aunt Sallie's woeful expression would have made any girl nervous. At the same time dark clouds had begun to appear overhead.

"You'd better get out the rain things," Ruth conceded. "I can't get this fixed very soon. Queer no one passes along this way. It's a lonesome kind of road. I wonder if we are off the main track?"

"It is a country lane, not a main road. I saw that at once," said Miss Sallie.

"Then why didn't you tell us, Aunt Sallie?"

"My eyes were closed to avoid the dust," replied Aunt Sallie firmly.

Poor Ruth had a task on her hands. If only the car had not skidded into that ugly hole, she could have managed; but it was impossible for her, with the help of all the girls, to lift the car enough to slip the new tire over the rim.

Mollie and Grace were taking Miss Sallie a little walk through the woods at the side of the road to try to make the time pass and to give Ruth a chance. Grace had winked at her slyly as they departed.

"Barbara," Ruth said finally, in tragic tones, "I'm in a fix and I might as well confess it. I know it all comes of my boasting that I didn't need a man. My kingdom for one just for a few minutes! Do you suppose there is a farmhouse near where we could find some one to help me get this wheel out of the rut? I'd surrender this job to a man with pleasure."

"I don't believe we are on the right road, Ruth, dear." Barbara felt so responsible that she was almost in tears. Ominous thunder clouds were rolling overhead, and Bab tried not to notice the large splash of rain that had fallen on her nose.

"Don't worry Bab, dear," urged Ruth. "I should have looked out for the road, too. It can't be helped."

"But I am going to help. You can just rely on that," announced Barbara, shaking her brown curls defiantly. She had taken off her hat in the exertion of trying to help Ruth. "We passed a sleepy-looking old farm a little way back, but I am going to wake it up!"

She heard Miss Sallie and the girls returning to the shelter of the car, for the rain had suddenly come down in torrents. Down the road sped Bab, shaking her head like a little brown Shetland pony.

Miss Sallie was in the depths of despair.

"Child," she said sternly to Ruth, "get into the car out of that mud. We will remain here, under the shelter of the covers until morning. Then, if we are alive, I myself will walk to the nearest town and telegraph your father. We will take the next train back to New

On Came Barbara, Riding Bareback.
[illustration from the 1910 edition]

York." Miss Sallie spoke with the extreme severity due to a rheumatic shoulder that had been disregarded.

"Please let me keep on trying, Aunt Sallie," pleaded Ruth. "I'll get the tire on, or some one will come along to help me. I am so sorry, for I know it is all my fault."

"Never mind, Ruth; but you are to come into this car." And Ruth, covered with mud, was obliged to give in.

"Where, I should like to know," demanded Miss Sallie, "is Barbara?"

Through the rain they could hear the patter, patter of a horse's hoofs.

"Cheer up, Ruth, dear," whispered Grace. "What difference does a little rain make? Here is some one coming along the road!"

Ruth's eyes were full of tears; Aunt Sallie's threat to stop their trip was more than she could bear; but she was soon smiling.

"Why, Barbara Thurston," the girls called out together, "it can't be you!" On came Barbara, riding bareback astride an old horse, the animal's big feet clattering, its mane and tail soaked with rain.

"Great heavens!" said Miss Sallie, and closed her eyes.

Barbara rode up to the automobile, her hand clasped tightly in the horse's mane.

"I'm as right as can be, Miss Sallie. I went back to that sleepy old farm, knocked and knocked for help, and called and called, but nobody would answer. Just as I gave up all hope, old Dobbin came to the porch and neighed, as if inquiring what I was doing on his premises. Like a flash I put out my hand, as though to pat him, grabbed him by the mane, hopped up here, and now you see the best lady bareback rider from Rinkhem's Circus. I led you into this mess; now I'm going to get you out. I shall ride old Dobbin into town and come back with help." Bab declaimed this, ending out of breath.

"Never mind, Miss Sallie," Mollie explained, seeing her consternation. "Bab never rode any other way than bareback when she was a little girl. Do let her go!"

"Very well; but she may be arrested as a horse thief. That is all I have to say in the matter." Miss Sallie sank back on her cushions, but Barbara had clattered off before she could be forbidden to go. She caught the words, "horse thief," as she rode as fast as old Dobbin would carry her.

"It's Barbara to the rescue again!" Ruth shouted after her.

CHAPTER VIII

"For We Are Jolly Good Fellows!"

"Suppose I should be arrested!" thought Barbara uncomfortably. "It would be distinctly unpleasant to be hauled off to jail, while Aunt Sallie and the girls remain stuck in the mud, not knowing my fate, and helpless to save me! I may meet old Dobbin's owner at any minute!"

It was after six o'clock, and, because of the heavy storm, was almost dusk. Barbara had decided to go to the end of the lane and find the main road to New Haven, hoping to sooner discover help in that direction.

Before long she came to a fork in the road. By riding close to the sign-post she found a hand pointing: "Nine Miles to New Haven." On she sped through the mud and rain, slipping and sliding on the horse's back, but still holding tight to his mane.

"Stop! Hello, there! Why, Mirandy, if that ain't my own hoss, and that girl astride it running off as fast as she can! Hello! Stop!" The farmer lashed the horse hitched to his rickety old buggy, and dashed after

Barbara, who had ridden past without noticing them. "Stop, thief!"

Down to her wet toes sank Barbara's heart. The worst she had feared had happened. If only she had seen their buggy in time to stop first and ask their help. Now, rushing by them, how could she explain? Horse thief, indeed.

"Oh, please," she said, her voice not quite steady, "I am not exactly running away with your horse; I am only going for help! My friends——"

The farmer grabbed the horse savagely by the mane. "Come on," he said. "You can tell your story at the nearest police station. I ain't got time fer sech foolishness. What I see, I see with my own eyes. You're plain running away with my hoss!"

"John," pleaded the farmer's wife, "you might listen to the young lady."

But Barbara's looks were against her. The rain had beaten her hair down over her eyes. Her clothes were wet and covered with mud from trying to help Ruth. What could she do? Barbara was frightened, but she kept a cool head. "I'll just let the old man haul me before the nearest magistrate. I expect *he'll* listen to me!" She was shivering, but she knew that to think bravely helped to keep up one's courage. "If only it were not so awful for Aunt Sallie and the girls to be waiting there, I could stand my part," murmured Bab.

For fifteen minutes captors and girl jogged on. Only the old man talked, savagely, under his breath. He wanted to get home to his farmhouse and supper, but this made him only the more determined to punish Barbara.

"I suppose we'll take all night to get to town at this rate," she thought miserably.

For we are jolly good fellows,
For we are jolly good fellows!

Barbara could hear the ring of the gay song and the distant whirr of a motor car coming down the road. If only she could attract someone's attention and make them listen to her! She could now see the lights of the automobile bearing down upon them.

Like a flash, before the farmer could guess what she was doing, Barbara whirled around on old Dobbin's back, and sat backwards. She put one hand to her lips. "Oh, stop! Stop, please!" she cried, looking like a gypsy, with her rain-blown hair and brown cheeks, which were crimson with blushes at her awkward position.

On account of the rain, and the oncoming darkness, the car was going slowly. At the end of one of the choruses the song stopped half a second. One of the young fellows in the car caught sight of Barbara, evidently being dragged along by the irate farmer and his wife.

"Hark! Stop! Look! Listen! Methinks, I see a female in distress," the young man called out.

The car stopped almost beside the buggy, and one of the boys in the car roared with laughter at Barbara's appearance, but the friend nearest him gave a warning prod.

"Hold on there!" called the first young man. "Where are you dragging this young lady against her will?"

"She's a hoss thief!" said the old man sullenly.

"I am no such thing," answered Barbara indignantly. Then, without any warning, Barbara threw back her head and laughed until the tears ran down her cheeks, mingling with the rain. It was absurdly funny, she sitting backwards on an old horse, one hand in his mane, and the farmer pulling them along with a rope. What must she look like to these boys? Barbara saw they were gentlemen, and knew she had nothing more to fear.

"Do please listen, while I tell my story. I am not a horse thief! I've some friends up the road, stuck in the mud with a broken tire in their automobile. I saw this old horse in the farm-yard, and I borrowed or rented him, and started for help. The old man wouldn't let me explain. Won't you," she looked appealingly at the four boys in their motor car, "please go back and help my friends?"

"Every man of us!" uttered one of the young fellows, springing up in his car. "And we'll drag this old tartar behind us with his own rope! We'll buy your old horse from you, if this young lady wants him as a souvenir."

It was the farmer's turn to be frightened.

"I am sure I beg your pardon, miss," he said, humbly enough now. His wife was in tears.

"Oh, never mind him," urged Barbara. "Please go on back as fast as you can to my friends. You'll find them up the lane to the left. I'll ride the old horse back to the farm, and settle things and join you later."

"Excuse me, Miss Paul Revere," disputed a tall, dark boy with a pair of laughing blue eyes that made him oddly handsome, "you'll do no such thing. Kindly turn over that fiery steed to me, take my seat in the car and show these knights-errant the way to the ladies in distress. I want to prove to you that a fellow can ride bareback as well as a girl can."

But the farmer was anxious to get out of trouble.

"I'll just lead the hoss back myself," he said. "No charge at all, miss." Evidently afraid of trouble, the farmer made a hurried start homeward, and was soon lost to view, while Barbara rode back to her friends with help.

In ten minutes two motor cars were making their way into New Haven. The passengers had changed places. Ruth sat contentedly with her hands folded in her lap, by the side of a masculine chauffeur, who had introduced himself as Hugh Post, and turned out to be the roommate, at college, of Mrs. Cartwright's brother, Donald. Barbara, wrapped in steamer rugs, sat beside the boy with the dark hair and blue eyes, whom Miss Sallie had recognized as Ralph Ewing, son of the friends with whom they expected to board at Newport.

It was arranged that Barbara and Ruth were to sleep together the first night at New Haven. The truth was, they wanted to talk things over, and there were no connecting doors between the three rooms. The hotel was an old one, and the rooms were big and dreary. They were connected by a narrow private hall, opening into the main hall by a single door, just opposite Ruth's and Barbara's room. The automobile girls were in a distant wing of the hotel, but the accommodations were the best that could be found.

Miss Sallie bade their rescuers a prompt farewell on arrival at the hotel. "We shall be delighted to see you again in the morning," she said, "but we are too used up for anything more to-night."

Barbara was promptly put to bed. She was not even allowed to go down to supper with the other girls, but lay snuggled in heavy covers, eating from a tray by her bed. Once or twice she thought she heard light footfalls outside in the main hall, but she had noticed a window that opened on a fire escape, and supposed that one of the hotel guests had walked down the corridor to look out of this window.

In a short time Ruth came back and reported that the automobile girls, including Miss Sallie, were ready for bed.

"I am not a bit sleepy. Are you?" Ruth asked Barbara. "I will just jump in here with you, so we can talk better. We've certainly had enough adventures for one day!"

"Oh, no!" replied Barbara; "I feel quite wide awake." Five minutes later both girls were fast asleep.

CHAPTER IX

Only Girls

Barbara and Ruth both awoke with a feeling that a light had flashed over their faces, but neither of them spoke nor moved. How long they had slept they could not know. It seemed almost morning, but not a ray of daylight came through the closed blinds.

Across the room the flash shone for an instant, then darted on like a will-o'-the-wisp. Both girls dimly saw the outline of a man crouching in the shadow along the wall. His hand slid cautiously up the sides of the bureau, fingering, for a moment, the toilet articles on the dresser. Then the search-light for an instant darted along the mantel and turned to the bed again. The girls were nearly fainting with terror. Ruth remembered that, for once, she had locked her money and her jewels in her trunk.

The man stood absolutely still and listened. Not a sound!

So quiet lay both girls that neither one knew the other had wakened.

The man continued his search, but plainly this was

not the room he sought. Still moving, his feet making absolutely no sound, the dark figure with the lantern crept out of the girls' room, to the front of the corridor, and turned down the narrow, private hallway.

"Aunt Sallie!" Ruth thought with a gasp. She had said she would leave her door open, so she might hear if the girls called her in the night. And Aunt Sallie carried a large sum of money for the expenses of the trip, and her own jewelry as well.

It may be that Ruth made a sound, anyway Barbara knew that her roommate was awake. Both had the same thought at just the same instant.

Noiselessly, without a word, on bare feet, both girls sped down the hall to Miss Sallie's open door. What they would do when they got there neither of them knew. It was time for action, not for thought! At the open door they paused and knelt in the shadow. Black darkness was about them, save in Aunt Sallie's room, where a dark lantern flashed its uncanny light. The girls were alert in every faculty. Now they could see more distinctly the form of the man who carried the lantern. He was of medium height and slender. Over his face he wore a black mask through which gleamed his eyes, narrowed to two fine points of steel.

Should the girls cry out? The man was armed and it might mean death to Aunt Sallie or themselves.

Evidently the burglar meant to make a thorough search of the room before he went to the bed, where, he guessed, the valuables were probably kept; but he must know first. The room was bare of treasure. He walked cautiously to where Miss Sallie still slept in complete unconsciousness, this time holding his lantern down, that its light should not waken the sleeping woman.

As he drew near her Ruth could bear the suspense no longer. She saw him drag out a bag from under Miss Sallie's head and could not refrain from uttering a low cry. It was enough. The man dashed the lantern to the ground and made a rush for the door.

There was no time for Ruth and Barbara to plan. They were only girls; but as the man ran toward them in the darkness, striking out fiercely, Barbara seized one of his legs, Ruth the other. Together, the three of them went down in the blackness. The girls had not the robber's strength, but they had taken him by surprise and they meant to fight it out.

He kicked violently to free himself, then turned and tore at Barbara's hands, but she clung to him. He raised the butt end of his pistol and struck with all his force. As the blow fell with a terrific thud, Barbara relaxed her hold, and tumbled over in the darkness.

By this time Miss Sallie realized what was happening. Yet, in the darkness, she could only cry for help, and moan: "Let him alone, girls! Let him go!"

With one leg free it seemed a simple task to get away. The noises were arousing the sleeping hotel guests. Another minute, and the burglar knew that he would be lost! With a violent wrench he tore himself away, and started down the hall, Ruth after him. If she could delay him a few seconds help would come!

The outside door leading from their private hall into the main one was nearly closed; in reaching to open it there was a second's delay. Ruth flung herself forward, caught the man's coat and clung desperately, but the burglar was too clever for her. In less than a second he slipped out of his coat, ran quickly to the window leading to the fire escape, and was gone! When assistance arrived, Ruth was standing in the front hall holding a man's coat in her hand.

"Oh, come!" she said in horror. "A light, please! Aunt Sallic has been robbed, and I am afraid Barbara has been killed!"

Ten or twelve people came running down the hall. The hotel proprietor and several servants made for the fire escape. Grace and Mollie, clad in kimonos, had joined Ruth in the hall, and were shaking with terror. Neither of them had spoken a word, but Grace silently handed Ruth her bath robe.

They turned and the three girls followed the rescuers, who were hastening toward Aunt Sallie's room. That elderly woman had already risen, struck a light and was in her kimono.

Barbara was leaning against a chair, white as a sheet, but unhurt!

"O Bab!" said Ruth, flying toward her, forgetting everything else in her relief, "I thought you were killed!"

"I thought so, too," nodded Barbara, calmly smiling,

as she reached for one of the blankets and wrapped herself in its folds, "but I wasn't. When the burglar raised the end of his pistol to strike me, I knew what was coming and ducked. He struck the side of the chair, and I tumbled over under it."

The hotel proprietor came into the room carrying a chamois bag.

"Madam," he asked, "is this your property? I found it outside here. Evidently the man dropped it in trying to make his escape. I cannot understand what has happened. The hotel is securely locked. The fire escape goes down into a closed court. The man could not have made his way down five stories, without being seen when we reached the window. It is incredible!"

By this time the halls were swarming with frightened visitors.

Grace had gone out to speak to them, and came in holding the burglar's coat in her hand. "How curious!" she said, handing the garment to the proprietor. "This is a gentleman's coat. I can tell by the lining and the whole appearance of it. It was not worn by a common thief!"

"Ruth, my child, and Barbara," said Aunt Sallie, when everyone had left their apartments, "I shall never forgive you!"

"Why not, Aunt Sallie?" both girls exclaimed, at once.

"Because, my dears, you didn't just scream and let the wretch escape at once. In my day girls would never have behaved as you did!"

"But, Aunt Sallie," protested Ruth, "the jewels and money are both safe, and neither Barbara nor I am hurt. I don't see how we could have done any better, even in your day."

"Kiss me," said Aunt Sallie, "and go back to bed at once. It is nearly morning."

When Mr. and Mrs. Cartwright drew up in front of the New Haven hotel, at a little after two o'clock next day, they found Miss Sallie and the four girls surrounded by a circle of college boys. With them stood a policeman.

"What has happened?" said Mrs. Cartwright in astonishment, jumping out of her car, as Donald Cartwright, Hugh Post and Ralph Ewing came down to meet her. "Are those my girls, to whom I am to introduce you to-day?"

"Goodness!" demanded Hugh. "Did you think we would wait twelve hours for an introduction! Do come and hear all that has happened."

Miss Stuart, looking a good deal shaken by her adventures, came forward to meet Mrs. Cartwright. "Listen!" she said dramatically, for Barbara was talking to the policeman.

"No, we would neither of us know him, because neither my friend nor I ever saw him before. It was dark and he was masked. But he was slight—not a big, rough kind of man—and his hands were soft, but strong as steel. I don't believe," she leaned over and whispered, "he could have been a servant, or an ordinary burglar."

"We have discovered, miss, that no entrance was made from the outside. Any guests who left the hotel this morning will be followed and examined. The chief will report to you later," the policeman said, with a low bow to Miss Sallie.

"Well, is this the way you see a nice, quiet, old college town?" Mrs. Cartwright inquired. "I suppose you mean to take the next train for home."

"No such thing!" retorted Ruth, smiling, and looking as bright and fresh as ever. "We don't mind a few weeny adventures, do we, Aunt Sallie?"

Miss Sallie held up her hands in horror. "Weeny adventures! What shall we expect next! However, I've promised the girls to go on. I think we need the trip, now, more than ever, and I want to ask Mr. Cartwright to keep the matter as quiet as possible. I do not wish my brother to know."

"Do please come on," said Hugh Post, turning to Ruth. "We are going," he explained, "out to the athletic grounds in our motor cars. The girls came to see the university, and we haven't shown them a blooming thing."

"We are going to the dance to-night, just the same," announced Mollie to Mrs. Cartwright. "Aunt Sallie is to rest this afternoon, so she will be equal to it. We wouldn't miss it for anything."

Mr. and Mrs. Cartwright joined the party, and, in a few minutes, the two motor cars had covered the two miles between the college campus and the thirty acres

Yale devotes to college sports. The visitors saw the athletic grounds thoroughly; here the football champions of the world had been trained, and there was the baseball diamond.

"Ralph's the crack oarsman of the lot," said Donald Cartwright; "but—great Scott! We can't show these girls anything, after the way they tackled the burglar last night."

"We'll get up a regatta in your honor, if you'll come again next year, Miss Thurston," said Ralph.

Barbara only laughed at him. "Look out," she warned. "I may make you keep your promise."

"Barbara," said Mollie that night, as they were getting ready for the dance which was to take place in the Old Alumni Hall, "are you sure you feel well enough for the ball to-night?"

"Nonsense, child, why shouldn't I? I feel as fine as a fiddle. It isn't doing things that uses one up, even tackling a burglar; it is thinking about them. Ruth and I didn't have any time to think about our burglar."

"Well," said Mollie, a little wistfully, smoothing the folds of her muslin dress, "I don't believe I am as anxious to go to the dance as I thought I was. Does this dress look *very* shabby? I wouldn't go, now, only it seems kind of hateful of me to refuse Mrs. Cartwright's invitation."

"Now, Molliekins," Barbara answered quite seriously, "it's your dress, isn't it? Of course, I have thought about mine, too. These are just simple muslins that we have worn before; but, when we left home, we neither of us dreamed we would go to a party in them. Let's just make the best of things. Anyhow, I've made up my mind to one thing, and I wish you would, too. You and I must not worry about being poor while we are on this trip. Let us not pretend that we are rich, because everybody we meet seems to be. Ruth knows we are poor, knows about our little cottage and not keeping a servant, and she doesn't mind. I don't believe really nice people care whether young girls are rich or poor, if they happen to like them. I don't mean to preach." Barbara put her arm around Mollie and waltzed her around the room. "Let us pretend we are both Cinderellas before the arrival of the fairy godmother."

Mollie didn't answer; but she tucked some pink roses in her belt. "It doesn't really matter about me, anyway," she decided. "I can't expect these grown-up boys to dance with me. I will just stay by Miss Sallie."

"All right, little Miss Wall-flower," laughed Bab, as she pinned on a knot of blue that Ralph Ewing had asked her to wear, as a tribute to the Yale colors.

It was Mollie, after all, who was the belle of the party. Perhaps this was because the other girls whispered to their partners that Mollie was afraid nobody would dance with her; or, perhaps, because she was the youngest, and the best dancer among them all.

"I am going to take this little lady under my special protection at Newport," Mrs. Cartwright said to Miss Stuart, late that evening. "I don't mean my 'butterfly girl' to be losing her beauty sleep."

Mollie looked at her "lovely lady" with eyes as blue as myrtle blossoms. Mrs. Cartwright was so exquisite, so young and so wealthy, she seemed to Mollie to have stepped out of a book.

Miss Sallie was vainly trying to collect her four charges all at once, in order to take them home.

"Aunt Sallie," Hugh Post said roguishly, as that lady made a last determined stand, and gathered her girls together, "you know, from your experience yesterday, that Miss Ruth can't handle a motor car, even though she can tackle a burglar. So we are going to follow you in my automobile to-morrow and see that you get to New London all right."

"Oh, no, you're not," protested Ruth. "This I will have you know is an automobile girls' excursion and nary a man allowed."

"This one time, kindly permit us to follow you at a respectful distance, won't you?" Hugh urged. "It's only a short trip to New London. To tell you the truth, the governor's yacht is over there and I hope to be able to persuade you to go aboard. It is not disrespectful of me, Miss Stuart, to speak so of my father; he was once governor of the state, and he rather likes to be reminded of it. Mother has a number of friends on board the yacht, and we shall be cruising up to Newport in a few days. I think it would be jolly for father and mother to know you."

CHAPTER X
Enter Gladys and Mr. Townsend

"Why, Gladys Le Baron, this is a surprise!" gayly said Grace Carter next afternoon, when the two parties of girls and men had left their automobiles and had come aboard Governor Post's yacht, the "Penguin," that lay just outside the New London harbor.

Grace was awaiting her turn to be introduced to her host and hostess, when she spied Gladys, in a pale blue flannel suit and a cream felt hat, strolling down the deck, looking very much at home.

"How ever did *you* get here?" queried Grace, smiling.

Gladys gave Grace's cheek an affected peck with her lips.

"I have a better right to ask that question of you," Gladys pouted, "only I am not surprised. Harry Townsend came over from New Haven, yesterday, and told me you had arrived the night before. He went over with Hugh for the dance, but I didn't feel like going, so he came back early yesterday morning. I am amazed Hugh did not speak of it to you."

"Oh, Mr. Post didn't know we had ever heard of

Harry Townsend, or you either. We met most unexpectedly, and we had plenty of excitement of our own. I must tell you about it."

At this moment, Hugh came over for Grace to introduce her to his mother.

"This is Miss Carter, mother," he said. "Will you introduce her to Mrs. Erwin and father? She seems to know Gladys already."

Harry Townsend had seen the newcomers, and came forward to speak to them with his most charming manner.

"Say, Townsend," challenged Hugh, "what made you run away from us? We thought, of course, you'd stay over for the dance. Thought that was your plan in going over to New Haven."

Harry turned to Miss Stuart. "I heard of your arrival in New Haven, the other evening," he said. "The fellows told me of your experiences; but I got away from the hotel too early next morning to pay my respects."

"Then you didn't hear of the burglar, did you?" queried Hugh.

In spite of Miss Sallie's protestations the whole story had to be gone over again.

Barbara was talking to Ralph Ewing and had not looked at Harry Townsend during the conversation, until he came over to speak to her.

"I have half an idea, Miss Thurston," he said, "that you do not like me, and I am sorry. I was looking forward to our having good times together at Newport, as

I am to be Mrs. Erwin's guest, with your cousin Miss Le Baron. Mrs. Post asked us on for the yacht trip a day or two sooner than we expected. We are all going up to Newport together."

"Mr. Townsend," said Barbara, her usually laughing, brown eyes now steadfast and serious, "I wonder why you think I do not like you?"

"Miss Stuart," begged Mrs. Post, after the governor had conducted the party over his trim little craft, "you must stay and dine with us on board the yacht to-night. I refuse to take no for an answer. I wish I could keep you over until morning, but unfortunately the yacht is too small."

Miss Sallie protested. No; they couldn't think of it. They had come aboard only for a call, and must get back to their hotel before night. But Hugh swept all her arguments aside. He was an adored only son, and accustomed to having his own way. To tell the truth, Miss Sallie was not averse to the idea of staying; it was pleasant to be meeting Newporters in advance. Miss Stuart was a woman who thought much of appearances, and of this world's goods, and their new acquaintances seemed to have plenty of both.

"It's an ill wind," she thought to herself, "and I must say, for my young niece, that she has a habit of falling on her feet."

But aloud Miss Sallie accepted the invitation with much decorum.

On the deck aft, where the young people had gathered, there was much laughter.

Gladys was really pleased to see Ruth. As for her cousins, they were a bore, but she had no idea of being openly rude to them. She simply meant to ignore them.

It was not easy to disregard two such popular girls. Barbara and Mollie seemed to be well able to get on without her patronage. Barbara was already smiling and chattering with Governor Post, while the boys described her mad ride of two days before.

"Father," said Hugh, "I forgot to introduce you to Miss Thurston by her proper title, 'Miss Paul Revere.'"

"Harry," asked Gladys, as they stood on the outside of the circle, "don't you think it is disgusting the way that forward cousin of mine always manages to put herself before the public?"

"Well," said Mr. Townsend—was there a little admiration in his tone?—"she seems to have plenty of grit."

It was really Mollie, not Barbara, who saw through Gladys's treatment of them. Barbara was too openhearted and boyish to notice a slight, unless it was very marked.

Gladys had asked Ruth and Grace to her stateroom, and Mrs. Post had put the other two girls into her unoccupied guest chamber. It was a little gem of a stateroom, upholstered in pale green to relieve the glare from the water.

"Bab," Mollie chuckled, rubbing her cheeks until they were pink, "do you remember the story of 'The Water Baby'?"

"Yes," Bab answered absently; "I do, after a fashion. But why do you ask? You haven't turned into a water baby, have you, just because you are on board a yacht for the first time in your life?"

"No," laughed Mollie. "I was thinking of the story in it of the salmon and the trout. Have you forgotten it?"

"Of course I have," admitted Barbara.

Mollie chuckled gleefully. "Our high and mighty cousin, Gladys, reminds me very much of the salmon, who thought the trout a very common fish, and disliked him all the more because he was a relation. Feel like a trout, Bab?"

"Not at all, Mollie; but do hurry and go out on deck. That young freshman, who came down in the automobile with us to amuse you, is wandering around outside, looking frightened to death. You must go and talk to him."

As Barbara stepped into the big salon, which was fitted up like a library, she saw one of the young men disappear quickly through the open door. Bab went over to their wraps, which they had dropped in a heap on a couch when they boarded the yacht, and selected her own jacket. Ruth's pocketbook was in full view among their belongings, and Bab covered it over before she went on deck.

Before dinner ended the moon had risen, the pale crescent hanging like a slender jewel in the sky.

Barbara was standing alone, for a second, when Mrs. Erwin approached her.

"Pardon me, dear," she said, "but did you or your sister see a small pin on the dressing table of the guest room, when you went in there before dinner? I have misplaced a ruby and diamond circle of no great value. I went into the guest chamber this morning, while the maid was cleaning my room, and I thought perhaps I had laid it down in there."

"No," said Bab, frowning. It did seem curious how losses were following them! "I didn't look, although it was probably there. I am most unobservant. I will ask my sister."

"No, no," said Mrs. Erwin, hastily; "please don't. I shall probably find it again. I don't want Mrs. Post to hear."

The next morning, when Grace and Ruth were donning their best motor veils and coats, Ruth suddenly looked surprised and began to search hurriedly through her pocketbook.

"Grace," she said, "I can't find fifty dollars. I am sure I had it yesterday, because I looked carefully after that wretched burglar had gone, though I knew all my money was safe in my trunk. Now it's gone!"

Ruth turned her pocketbook upside down. "Don't tell Aunt Sallie, please," she begged. "I don't know what she would say to have this item added to our adventures."

Miss Sallie's voice was heard calling from the next room.

"Girls, are we or are we not, going to Newport to-day? I, for my part, wish to spend no more time on the way!"

CHAPTER XI

Newport at Last!

The automobile girls were in a flutter of excitement. Another half hour, and they would arrive in Newport!

"Ruth," said Miss Sallie, "slow up this car a little! Before we enter Newport, I must see to my appearance. To think of all I have gone through since I left Kingsbridge!" Miss Sallie took out a small hand mirror, thoughtfully surveying her own unwrinkled face. "What will you children get me into before we are through with this trip?"

Ruth slowed down obediently.

"Open my bag, Mollie," said Miss Sallie, decidedly, "and you, Grace, look under the seat for my other hat. We shall probably arrive in Newport at five o'clock, the hour for the fashionable parade. I, at least, shall do what I can to give our car an appearance of gentility. I advise you children to do the same."

"Would you like a little cold cream, Miss Sallie, to wipe off your face?" Mollie spoke timidly, remembering how Barbara had laughed at her.

"Certainly I should, my child, and very intelligent of you to have brought it along."

"Well," said Ruth, "if you must 'fix up,' and I am to take a party of belles and beauties into Newport, instead of true lovers of sport, there are lots of new veils under my seat. Bab, take them out and pass them around. Only the chauffeur shall be dusty and dilapidated enough to look the part."

Behold their dream had come true! The automobile girls were at last in Newport, watching the summer parade!

Ruth, at the expected hour, turned her car, with a great flourish, into Bellevue Avenue, Newport's most fashionable thoroughfare. For a few minutes the girls beheld a long procession of carriages and automobiles; a little later, they swung round a corner and stopped in front of a beautiful old Colonial house, with a wide veranda running around three sides of it, and a hospitably open front door.

Miss Sallie descended first, to be greeted by Ralph's mother, who was expecting them.

"I don't like her. She's not a bit like Ralph," thought Barbara. Then she gave herself an inward shake. "There, Barbara, you know what mother would say to you about your sudden prejudices!"

Mrs. Ewing, who had been a great beauty in her day, looked as though life had disagreed with her.

Barbara had wondered how a private home could accommodate so many people, never having seen a handsome old New England house, but their three rooms occupied only half of one side of the long hall on the second floor. "And they think they are poor!" smiled Bab, to herself, as she looked admiringly at the handsome furniture. "I wonder what they would think of our little five-room cottage."

"I want some clean clothes before anything else," sighed dainty Mollie, standing before a mirror, gazing with disdain at her own appearance. "I believe I have one clean shirtwaist left, but I must still wear this dusty old skirt."

But Ruth was staggering into the room under an immense box.

"Fifteen dollars express charges, mum; not a cent less! Them's my orders. And extry for carrying the box upstairs. It ain't my business. I'm too accommodating I am! Where shall I put it down, mum?"

Ruth dropped the heavy bundle on the bed; she couldn't carry it a moment longer.

"Why, Ruth Stuart!" said Mollie, dancing with glee. "It's some clothes for us! How did mother get them here in such a hurry? Oh, joy! oh, rapture! I was just fussing about having to wear this old suit to-night."

Bab was tugging at the heavy cords.

"Foolish Bab!" scoffed Ruth. "You'll never get it open that way," and she cut the cord in a business-like fashion with a little knife she always carried.

"Now I'll run away and leave you," Ruth continued. "Grace is calling that it is time for my bath.

Your turn next. I'll see the pretty things when I come back."

Ruth would like to have stayed to see the girls open the box, but she had an instinctive feeling that they would prefer to be alone.

"Here's a letter from mother. Let's read that first," said Bab.

Inside the letter lay two crisp ten-dollar bills!

"I have had a windfall, children," the letter read, "through the kindness of Mr. Stuart. He told me that some of my old stock that I thought of no value was paying a dividend again. Curiously, your Uncle Ralph had not mentioned it to me; but, when I wrote and told him of Mr. Stuart's advice, he sent it to me at once. So here's a little spending money. And oh, my darlings, I hope you will like your new clothes! Mr. Stuart is so kind to me, I am not lonely," the letter ended, "so have the best time you possibly can. I shall send your trunk to-morrow with your summer muslins and underwear."

"Mollie mine, don't tear the paper in that fashion," remonstrated Barbara. "Let me open the box. Behold and see!" She held up two dainty organdie frocks, delicate and airy. Mollie's gown was white, with little butterfly medallions of embroidery and lace sprinkled over it.

"Mollie, Mollie! How could mother have guessed your new name was 'the butterfly girl'? Isn't it too lovely!" Bab almost forgot to look at her own frock, so enraptured was she with her sister's.

But Barbara's frock was just as charming, and as well suited to her. A circle of pink wild roses outlined the hem and encircled the yoke, which was of delicate pink tulle.

Mollie was rummaging with impatient fingers. "Party capes, I do declare—the very newest style! I never reached the point of expecting capes even in my wildest dreams. See, yours is all white, and mine has a pale blue lining with a dear little 'blue riding hood cap.' Oh, won't I be charming?" murmured Mollie, putting the cape over her shoulders and pirouetting before the mirror. "Surely no sensible wolf would want to eat me up!"

Two light flannel suits, one of cream color for Bab, and a pin-stripe of blue and white for Mollie, completed the glories of the box.

"Now," said Bab, "what more can we want, for tennis, for rowing, for yachting, for driving? Are there any more entertainments that the rich enjoy, Mollie? Because, if there are, I should like to mention them."

Oh, the girls will all declare,
When they see me on the square—
Here comes a millionaire,
Mollie darling!

"What do you think of that for poetry made while you wait? You don't half appreciate my talents, Miss Mollie Thurston," ended Bab, with a final hug.

"Hurry, children," called Miss Sallie, appearing at

their door. "You know we are to meet Mrs. Cartwright at the Casino to-night. She wants to introduce us to the place where a large part of Newport's gayety occurs."

"What is the 'Casino'?" whispered Mollie, when Miss Sallie had disappeared.

"Oh, it's only a big club, where you play tennis and have dances, and any sort of entertainments. Nearly all the nicest people in Newport belong to it. Mrs. Cartwright says we'll have most of our fun over there."

Bab put her arm round her sister, as they walked downstairs.

"Mollie," she said, "I have the queerest feeling. I am so happy, it frightens me. I never had such a good time before. I wonder how it will all turn out?"

Barbara could not guess that there were to be tears for her, as well as joys, at Newport. It was as well she did not know, or her pleasure would have been marred.

The girls finished dinner as quickly as possible.

"There's time for a stroll on the cliffs, isn't there, before eight?" inquired Ruth. "Do you feel equal to exercise, Aunt Sallie? Everyone takes the cliff walk the first thing after arrival in Newport."

"Certainly," Miss Sallie agreed. "I suppose I can manage it, though I have ridden so far that I may have lost the use of my limbs. However, I can sit down if I grow tired, and you children can go on without me. It's perfectly safe, isn't it, Mrs. Ewing?"

"Oh, yes," Mrs. Ewing replied; "though it looks fairly

dangerous, the cliffs are so high, the highest on the Atlantic Coast from Cape Ann to Yucatan. But very few accidents have occurred there—so far."

Ruth and Barbara led the way. They could hear the sea booming and pounding below them. From the edge of the cliff they looked down a hundred feet at the sea, washing in on the level stretch of beach.

Ruth shivered and turned pale. "Oh," she shuddered, "it makes me horribly nervous! I am ashamed of it, so I don't often mention it, but I simply can't look down from great heights. It even makes me a little sick to look out of a high window, and I'm a miserable climber, I get so dizzy. Let us go back. Do you mind, Bab?"

"No, Ruth," Bab answered. "I suppose I am a tomboy; I used to play hare and hounds with the boys at school, and I learned to climb like a goat over the rocks at Kingsbridge; but these Newport cliffs are a different matter."

Barbara's powers were to be tested, but neither she nor Ruth thought anything more of their talk. Miss Sallie and the other two girls had joined them, and they made their way along the narrow, winding path that dipped in hollows and curves, and stretched for two miles ahead of them.

"How hard it is," said Miss Sallie, "to tell which view is the more beautiful!"

On the inland side of the cliffs, beautiful, shaded lawns, luxuriant with flowers, ran down to the edge of the path. Set in their midst were the marble palaces of

Newport's millionaires. Toward the sea, great points of land jutted out into the harbor, where the water was violet with the shadows of the closing day.

"Miss Stuart! Miss Stuart!" Aunt Sallie heard a gay voice calling her.

Running across the lawn, and waving her scarf at them, came Mrs. Cartwright.

"Were you coming to see me first?" she asked.

Miss Stuart confessed that she had not the shadow of an idea which house belonged to Mrs. Cartwright.

"You must see it for a minute, since you are already here," urged Mrs. Cartwright, and led the way up the graveled path to her veranda.

"Mollie," she said, addressing the young girl, "I think it is peculiarly appropriate for my butterfly girl to be introduced to my piazza. It is made to look like a Japanese teahouse," she explained to Miss Sallie.

The sides of Mrs. Cartwright's veranda were of heavy Japanese paper stretched on bamboo poles which opened and closed at will. The paper had been painted by a famous Japanese artist to represent springtime in Japan. There were whole rows of cherry trees in full blossom, with little Japanese children playing beneath them. Opposite this scene was another painting—a marshy lake, surrounded by queer Japanese birds.

The veranda was lighted by a hundred tiny shaded lamps. Japanese matting covered the floor, while the tea tables were set with tea services bought in old Japan. The girls had never seen anything so lovely.

"You are officially invited to have tea with me here, any or every afternoon you are in Newport. Now I will run and get Mr. Cartwright," added their hostess, "and we will go over to the Casino."

Outside, the Casino looked like a rambling, old Dutch mansion, with peaked gables and overhanging eaves.

"We've a Dutch house, English lawns and a French chef," Mr. Cartwright laughingly explained to Miss Sallie as they entered.

"And we've dozens of tennis courts," added Mrs. Cartwright. "We are working dreadfully hard, now, for the tournament that is to take place in a few weeks. It is really the social event of the whole year at Newport. Is there a star player among you girls? Why not enter the tournament and compete for the championship? We are to have a special match game, this year, played by the young people. Let us keep these tennis courts busy for a while. You'll come over, too, Miss Stuart, won't you, and play bridge while we work. Or you'll work at bridge, while we play tennis. Perhaps you think that is the way I should have put it."

CHAPTER XII

A Week Later

"Barbara, I wouldn't play tennis with Gladys and Harry Townsend, if I were you," said Mollie to her sister, one morning a week later. "They were horrid to you yesterday. Didn't you notice, when you called to Hugh and Ruth that their last ball had gone over the line, Gladys just shrugged her shoulders, and gave a sneery kind of smile to that Townsend fellow, and he lifted his eyebrows! Is your score the best, or Ruth's? I know you're both ahead of Gladys and Grace. I am sure Gladys doesn't play a bit better than I do; so she needn't have been so high and mighty."

Mollie shrugged her dainty shoulders. "You see, she told me, the first day she arrived, that, of course, I didn't play in the class with the others, so you had just the right eight for the two courts—four girls and four men."

"Why, Mollie!" Bab looked surprised. "I thought you said you didn't want to play. You can take my place any time."

Mollie smiled. "No," she answered; "I don't want to

play. It's not that. But it annoys me when you let Gladys Le Baron, cousin or no cousin, snub us all the time, and you not notice it. Ralph certainly wouldn't like to have me play with him now, when you're in for a match game."

"Mollie," said Bab, tying her tennis shoe, "I *do* notice how rude Gladys is. She left me standing all alone the other afternoon, when Ruth and Grace had gone into the club house to speak to Aunt Sallie. Friends of Gladys's came up, and she deliberately turned her back on me and didn't introduce me. I felt so out of it! Mrs. Post and Mrs. Erwin soon joined them, and they shook hands with me. I found the other people were some guests who had come down for Mrs. Erwin's ball, next week, and were staying at her house.

"I know," she continued, "Gladys is furious that we are invited to the dance. Mrs. Erwin was so cordial and nice. She said, right before me, that though the ball was a grown-up affair, she knew Gladys would want her cousins and friends, and she had invited us on her account. Wasn't it funny? Miss Gladys couldn't say a word. Goodness knows, *she* doesn't want us. She has been lording it over us, for days, because she and Harry were to be the only very young people invited. Gladys imagines herself a woman of society, and is in reality merely a foolish little girl," said Barbara. Then she added reflectively: "Miss Sallie says we are all too young to 'go out,' and she doubts the propriety of allowing us to attend Mrs. Erwin's ball. Last night she told Ruth she had almost decided against our going. Ruth championed our cause on the strength of the shortness of our stay in Newport, also that we should be permitted to go as a special favor to our hostess. You know Miss Sallie hates to refuse Ruth anything. Consequently we will be 'among those present' at Mrs. Erwin's ball whether Miss Gladys approves or not."

"I just wish I could tell my lovely Mrs. Cartwright how mean Gladys is," said Mollie. "She would not ask her to her charity fair."

"Please don't say anything, Mollie," pleaded Barbara, taking her tennis racquet from the bed. She had already answered Ralph's impatient whistle from the garden below. "It won't do any good for us to be horrid to Gladys in return; it will only make us seem as hateful as she is. Things will come around, somehow. I don't mind her—so very much."

"Well, I do," answered Mollie. "But you haven't told me how your score and Ruth's stand."

"Oh, I think we are pretty nearly even." Barbara was half way out the door. "Be careful, Molliekins," she urged, "if you go rowing with that freshman this afternoon. Why do you want to know about Ruth's score and mine? It's a week before the game, and anything may happen before then. We all play pretty evenly; Hugh Post and Ralph Ewing, too."

"Oh, I didn't mean anything, Bab," Mollie said, thoughtfully. "Only Ruth's awfully anxious to play in the tournament. She's just crazy about it."

"Of course she is, child. So are we all, for that matter," answered Bab. "You don't mean——"

"I don't mean a single thing, Bab Thurston!" said Mollie, a little indignantly.

"Yes, I am coming, at last, Ralph," Barbara sang softly over the banisters. She had not overcome her awe of Mrs. Ewing. Ralph's mother was by no means pleased with the idea that her adored Ralph preferred Barbara to any of the other girls.

"It's like Ralph," she complained to his father, "to pick out the poorest girl of the lot, when the rich ones are so much more charming. A great way for him to retrieve the family fortunes!"

"We will hope," said Ralph's father quietly, "that Ralph will not try to restore our fortunes by marrying for money."

As Barbara walked down to meet Ralph she looked grave, and her face was flushed. Ruth *did* want to play in the tournament, but so did she, for that matter! Could she resign in Ruth's favor? Then Barbara laughed to herself. "Catch a girl like Ruth letting me give up to her! I wonder if it would be fair of me to disappoint Ralph?"

"Come on, Miss Day-dreamer," ordered Ralph, hurrying her along. "The others have been waiting for us for fifteen minutes down at the Casino courts. Do you know that there is a party on for the afternoon? Ruth and Hugh are to pile as many of us as they can into their motor cars, and take us ten miles out the Ocean

Drive. We are to stop at Mrs. Duffy's English tea place on our way back."

Bab was certainly not playing in good form today. She even missed one of Gladys's serves, which were usually too soft to count. When the morning's practice was over, Ruth's and Hugh's score was two points ahead.

"Who is going to play in the tournament from these courts?" asked Mrs. Cartwright, crossing the lawn, her tennis racquet swinging in her hand. Mollie was close beside her, also "that freshman," who followed Mollie wherever she went.

"Bab," answered Ruth, coming up to smile at Mrs. Cartwright, who was looking prettier than usual in her tennis blouse of pale pink madras with a linen skirt of the same shade.

"What a funny Gladys!" Mrs. Cartwright laughed as the other girls joined her. "You are following our latest Newport fad, are you not, of having your head wrapped in a chiffon veil while you play tennis. You look like a Turkish girl, with only your eyes peeping out."

Gladys had tied up her head in a pale blue chiffon veil, with a fetching bow just over the ear. The other women who were playing on the courts, with the exception of Mrs. Cartwright and the automobile girls, were draped in the same fashion.

"That suggests a game to me," continued Mrs. Cartwright. "You must come to my veranda some night and we will play it. It is called 'eyeology.' I won't tell you anything more about it now. Just you wait! But to go back to my first question. Then I am to enter Barbara for the tournament?"

"I should say not, Mrs. Cartwright," said Barbara, who was standing near. This time she would not let Ruth speak.

"Ruth is certainly the best player among us," drawled Gladys; "she and Mr. Post; but," she went on in insinuating tones, "you know there are strange things that can happen in tennis!"

"If you mean, Gladys, that I cheated the other day," broke out Barbara fiercely, "I simply won't bear it! I know it is horrid of me to make a scene," she turned to Ruth with her eyes full of tears, "but this is the second time."

"Please don't get excited, Miss Thurston," cried Gladys scornfully. "I have not said you cheated. It looks a little bit like a case of guilty conscience."

Harry Townsend smiled knowingly.

Bab, nearly in tears, couldn't answer, but Ralph and Hugh Post both protested indignantly.

"Please don't discuss a thing of this kind here," said Mrs. Cartwright, angrily. "We don't allow quarreling on the Casino courts. I am surprised at you, Barbara. You were accused of nothing."

Mollie's eyes were black, instead of their usual lovely blue. She was very indignant, but she was always more of a diplomat than Barbara.

"Lovely lady," she said, putting her hand in Mrs.

Cartwright's as they moved away, "Gladys did mean that Bab cheated. This is the second time she has said it. Wouldn't you answer back if you were accused of not playing fair with your very best friend?"

Mrs. Cartwright gave Mollie's hand a squeeze. "Tell Barbara I am sorry if I was too hard on her, but I don't like scenes!"

"I wish I could get an excuse to pummel that Harry Townsend!" muttered Ralph indignantly to Hugh, when the girls had gone home. "I can't take it out on Gladys, for she's a girl. That Townsend fellow's nothing but a sneak. He just stands round and smiles and says nothing, until he puts me in a rage!"

"Oh, don't fight, Ralph," Hugh protested. "I hate that Townsend man, though, as much as you do. He is too infernally polite, for one thing, and he walks on his tiptoes. He comes right up behind you, and you never know where he is until he speaks. I believe he wears rubber soles on his shoes!"

That afternoon, when the automobile parties had finished drinking their tea, Barbara asked Ralph to take a little walk with her in the woods. She wanted to ask him something.

"Ralph," she began, "if I should fall down in my tennis, in the next few days, would you and Hugh play a test game to see which of you is the better man to help Ruth out in the tournament?"

Ralph shook his head. "No," he answered. "You are not losing your nerve, are you, Bab? Ruth and Hugh are wonderfully good players, but we are as good as the rest of 'em. I'll take my chances with you."

"Would you be very, very much disappointed if we lost?"

"Oh, yes," said Ralph, cheerily, "but I could bear it all right." He looked hard at Barbara for a minute. Then he said: "Go ahead, Barbara; I think I understand. I am game. And I'll never breathe it to a soul. Hugh and Ruth would never forgive us, if they found out!"

"Well, Ralph," said Barbara, "I don't think there's going to be any reason for my trying to let Ruth win; she's a better player than I am, and she will win anyhow, but, in case she shouldn't, Ruth has been a perfect dear to Mollie and me!"

"Gladys," said Ruth that night, when the young people were having an informal dance at the Casino, "I shall never forgive you for accusing Barbara of cheating, as you did today. Barbara is perfectly incapable of cheating. I can't understand why you don't like her."

Ruth's frank face clouded. She was incapable of understanding the petty meannesses in Gladys's nature.

"Mr. Townsend and I thought differently concerning Miss Thurston," Gladys replied, "but I have made no accusations, and will make none. You will find things out for yourself, though, when it is too late!"

Mollie was very sympathetic with Barbara that night. Things had not been going well with Bab for several days; she had an unfortunate habit of speaking her mind without thinking, and this trait had gotten her into trouble with Miss Sallie several times. That lady had a profound respect for the rich, while Barbara had been heard to say that some of the most fashionable ideas of Newport were "just nonsense."

"Bab," comforted Mollie, "Mrs. Cartwright told me to say she was sorry she had been cross to you. She wants you to be the gypsy fortune-teller at her bazaar. She says you are very clever, and would do it better than anyone else; besides, she thinks no one would know you. She has lots of gypsy things to dress up in."

"I would much rather be a waitress, like you girls," Bab declared.

"But you will do what Mrs. Cartwright wants you to, won't you?" urged Mollie.

"I'll see," said Bab.

The automobile girls were seeing Newport indeed! Mrs. Erwin and Mrs. Cartwright were both leaders in society. The girls had not only been invited to Mrs. Erwin's ball, but to the big dance which took place after the tennis tournament, and Mrs. Cartwright was arranging for a Charity Fair, which was to be the most original entertainment of the Newport season.

CHAPTER XIII

The Night of the Ball

"Yes, Hugh," Barbara said, as the last strains of the Merry Widow waltz died away, "I should like to rest here a minute." Barbara sank down on the low, rose-colored divan shaded by magnificent palms in Mrs. Erwin's conservatory. "I would love an ice, too," she added.

It was the night of Mrs. Erwin's famous white and gold ball, long remembered in the history of splendid entertainments in Newport.

Barbara truly wanted a minute to think. She had come to the ball under Miss Sallie's excellent chaperonage, early in the evening, and had been dancing hard ever since. The little girl from Kingsbridge, who had never before seen anything finer than a village entertainment, felt almost overcome by the splendor and magnificence of everything about her.

Mrs. Erwin's ballroom was built out from the side of her handsome villa like a Greek portico. The conservatory joined it at one end, forming an inner triangular court. This court was filled with rare trees which threw their branches out over a miniature artificial lake. The guests could pass from the ballroom into this open garden, or they could enter it through the conservatory.

The walls of the wonderful ballroom were covered with a white silk brocade, and on this night Mrs. Erwin had allowed only yellow flowers to be used as decorations. Great bowls of yellow roses perfumed the air, and golden orchids looked like troops of butterflies just poising before they took flight.

"Now I know," said Mollie, with a catch in her breath, as she first came into the magnificent ballroom, "what King Midas's garden must have looked like, when he went round and caressed all the flowers in it with the golden touch."

"Clever Mollie!" laughed Ruth. "I expect it is the golden touch that has been round this ballroom, or the touch of golden dollars, anyway."

Mollie blushed. "I didn't mean that," she said.

Barbara leaned her head against the rose-colored cushion, just the color of the jeweled spray in her hair; she was wearing the coral jewelry her mother had given her. Fortunately the two girls had saved their best party dresses for this ball, having been content to wear their summer muslins at the informal dances at the Casino.

Barbara, in her dainty pink flowered organdie, with her cheeks flushed to match it in color, resembled a lovely wild rose.

Curiously enough, amid all this elegance, Bab felt a

little homesick. She kept thinking of her mother and the little cottage.

"It's a wonderful experience for Mollie and me," she said to herself. "I hope I can tell mother exactly what it looks like. I am sure fairyland can't be half so gorgeous; fairies wear only dewdrops for jewels; but here, I believe, there must be nearly all the jewels in the world."

Barbara did not know how big the world really is, nor how many people and jewels, both real and paste, there are in it. After all, artificial people are no better than paste jewels!

Earlier in the evening Mollie and Barbara had stood with their hands tight together, watching the men and women enter the great reception room to speak to their host and hostess.

"Diamonds," whispered Mollie to Bab, "seem as plentiful as the strawberries we gathered for the hotel people this summer. We didn't dream, then, that we were coming to Newport! Isn't my Mrs. Cartwright the most beautiful of them all?" wound up the loyal child.

Mrs. Cartwright wore a white satin gown, with a diamond star in the tulle of her bodice. In her hair was a spray of diamonds, mounted to look like a single stalk of lilies of the valley, each jewel hanging from the slender stem like a tiny floweret.

The conservatory was almost empty while Bab rested and waited.

During the intermission in the dance nearly all the

guests had wandered into the dining-room or into the moonlit garden.

Barbara realized that she was almost completely hidden by the great palm trees that formed an arch over her head and drooped their long arms down over her. She had crept into this seat in order that she might see without being seen.

Yet in spite of the quiet, Barbara was not resting. Her heart was beating fast with the excitement of this wonderful evening, and her tiny feet in the pink silk slippers still kept time to the last waltz she had danced with Hugh.

The conservatory door, leading into the garden, was open. Barbara saw Mrs. Post, Governor Post, Harry Townsend and a woman in a gold-colored brocade enter the conservatory and stop to talk for a few minutes. They had not noticed Barbara nor did she feel it was quite proper to interrupt them, as she did not know the strange woman who was with them.

Governor Post bowed in military fashion to the ladies.

"Now," he said, "I'll go, and leave the young man to do the entertaining. We old fellows must make ourselves useful when our ornamental days are over. Mr. Townsend will look after you here, and I shall find a waiter and have him bring you something to eat."

Barbara saw Harry Townsend talking in his most impressive manner to the two women.

"It is curious," Bab thought, to herself, "what a society man Harry Townsend is. Gladys says he is only twenty-two. I wonder where he comes from. Nobody seems to know. Oh, yes; Gladys said he was educated in Paris. She met him on shipboard."

The little girl from her green bower was an interested watcher. It was fascinating to be able to see all that was going on, without being seen. Bab sat as quiet as a mouse, taking no part in the conversation.

Mrs. Post was a handsome woman of about fifty, who looked rather stern to the girls; but Hugh assured them that she was "dead easy," once you got on the right side of her. Her husband was a prominent lawyer in Washington, and their winters were usually spent in the capital.

Mrs. Post's gown was nearly covered by a long, light-colored chiffon wrap, with a high collar lined with a curious ornamental embroidery.

"Harry," she said, turning to the young man with her, "it is warm in here with these tropical plants; will you be kind enough to remove my wrap?"

The conservatory was dimly lighted. Barbara sat in the shadow. Between her and the party she was watching was a central row of flowers and evergreens, dividing the long room into two aisles.

She saw Harry rise and lean over Mrs. Post, who only half rose from her chair. Deftly and with wonderful ease and swiftness, Townsend undid the clasp at her throat; but, for a moment, the embroidery from the collar seemed to have caught in her hair.

Barbara's eyes grew wide and staring with surprise. As the coat slipped back from Mrs. Post's shoulders, she saw a string like a tiny green serpent glide with magic smoothness and swiftness from her throat, and drop into the shrubbery back of her, or—into Harry Townsend's hand?

What should she do? Announce that she had seen her string of emeralds disappear? Mrs. Post was talking and laughing gayly with her friend in the gold-colored dress. Harry was smiling quietly by them. Barbara rubbed her eyes. Surely she was mistaken. She had been dazzled by the wonderful sights she had seen that night. While she hesitated her opportunity passed.

Governor Post returned, saying to his wife: "Come, my dear, I have found Miss Stuart and a friend. They have a table out in the garden, and want us to join them."

Mrs. Post again drew her wrap over her shoulders and turned to leave the conservatory. As she rose she saw Barbara.

"You there, my child?" she said in a friendly way. "Why didn't you speak to me?"

Barbara could only answer her stupidly. "I was waiting for Hugh."

When Hugh returned he found Barbara looking as pale as though she had just seen a ghost.

"What's the matter?" he asked at once. "Are you ill?"

But Bab shook her head. "I'll go find Miss Stuart," the young man suggested.

"You'll do no such thing, Hugh!" Barbara had recovered her breath. "There's nothing much the matter with me—at least, I am not sure whether I ought to tell you."

"Bab and Hugh! Well, I like this!" Grace's voice sounded from the doorway, as she and Donald Cartwright came in, followed by Ruth and Ralph. "Here you two have run away by yourselves, when we promised to stick together this evening, in order to keep up each other's courage. You ought to see Gladys! She's as angry as can he, and is wandering round with Mollie and the freshman. Harry has been gone somewhere for a long time, and she has no partner for the next dance."

"Are you sick, Bab?" inquired Ruth. She, too, noticed that Bab was unusually pale. Before she received an answer, Governor and Mrs. Post came into the conservatory, followed by Harry Townsend, Miss Stuart and the woman in yellow.

"You are just the fellow I want to see, Hugh," said his father, so quietly that no one except those near him could hear. "Your mother has lost her emerald necklace, and she thought she had it on when she was last in here. We don't want to create any excitement, or to let Mrs. Erwin or the servants know until we have made a thorough search. She very probably dropped it among these flowers. Lock the door out there, will you? Miss Carter, you and Donald, please keep guard at the other door while these young people help me look."

"I thought——" said Barbara.

"Why, you were in here, child, when we were. You were on the other side of these evergreens," said Mrs. Post. "What did you say?"

"I thought it might be in these evergreens," Barbara finished, lamely, getting down on her knees to assist in the search. Dared she speak of what she thought she had seen? Dared she speak with no evidence but her own word? Could she have been in error? First, she would look with the others.

Every palm, every flower, every inch of space was carefully gone over. No sign of the missing emeralds!

"Did anyone enter the conservatory after I left, Miss Thurston?" inquired Mrs. Post coldly. She was worried by the loss of her jewels, which were of great value, as well as annoyed by the excitement she was causing.

"Nobody came in," Bab said, "only Hugh."

"I am exceedingly sorry," the governor said at last, "but Mrs. Erwin will have to be notified. The jewels were either lost or stolen, and must be found. If the servants find the necklace a liberal reward will induce them to return it."

The older people left the conservatory.

Just as the younger ones turned to leave, Barbara, whose strange expression had not escaped the sharp eyes of Ruth, laid her hand on Hugh's arm.

"Ask Harry Townsend to stay here a minute with us, won't you please, Hugh?" said Barbara hoarsely.

"Say, Townsend," Hugh called, "come back a moment. I want to speak to you. Or, rather, Miss Thurston does."

"Mr. Townsend," said Barbara, her face pale as death,

"did you not see Mrs. Post's necklace when you took off her wrap in here?"

"No," said Harry quietly. "Did you?"

"Ask him, Hugh," said Barbara, desperately, "to show you what he has in his pockets!"

"Oh, say, Barbara!" Hugh answered. "I can't do that. It's a little too much."

But Ralph stepped forward. "We don't know what Miss Thurston means, but she most certainly doesn't mean to insult Mr. Townsend unnecessarily. Why, then, should he mind turning out his pockets? Here Hugh," Ralph turned, "search me first. Then Mr. Townsend won't object to the selfsame process."

Hugh's face was crimson, but he looked through Ralph's pockets in a gingerly fashion.

When he finished Harry Townsend turned quietly to Barbara. "I don't know why you wish to insult me," he said to her, "but I am perfectly willing to have Mr. Post search me. You were the only person in the conservatory after the jewels were lost!"

Hugh started his search.

Barbara leaned sick and faint against her chair, expecting every moment to see Hugh draw the jewels forth. She kept her eyes averted while Harry turned his pockets wrong side out and finally opened his vest.

"Barbara," said Hugh, coldly, and Bab turned around. "We owe Mr. Townsend an apology. He is certainly no thief!"

The jewels were nowhere to be found.

· · · · · · · · · · · · ·

CHAPTER XIV

Barbara's Secret

"**B**ab, Bab! What is the matter with you!" cried Mollie, for Barbara had thrown herself on the bed after their return from the ball, bursting into a torrent of tears.

"Oh, I don't know," sobbed Bab. "I must be wrong, or crazy, or something. Yet how can people doubt their own eyes?"

Mollie stopped spreading out her butterfly dress, in which she had looked so pretty at the party, and flung her arms round her sister. "Just tell me what is the matter, dear! Has anyone hurt your feelings? If it's that Gladys Le Baron I'll certainly get even with her!"

But Bab didn't answer.

"I'm going to call Ruth," said Mollie. "I don't want to waken Aunt Sallie, but you seemed queer all the way home from the ball."

Bab sat up, when Ruth came in, and dried her eyes.

"I am so sorry you feel so badly, Barbara, dear," said Ruth, "but, of course, it was a wretched mistake for you to have made. Let's try to forget that horrid scene. Some servant will pick up the necklace in the morning, and return it to Mrs. Post. Hugh and I have decided that it will be wise for those of us who were in the conservatory just at the last not to speak of what happened. You will forgive us, Mollie, dear, won't you, if we don't tell even you?"

"No, I won't!" cried Mollie, stamping her little slippered foot. "Bab can't have secrets that make her cry— not from her own sister. And I don't see, anyway, what Bab has to do with Mrs. Post having lost her emerald necklace. If you think the loss is a secret, you're wrong, because everybody in the ballroom was whispering it about half an hour afterwards. I heard of it from a perfect stranger!"

"Mollie," said Ruth quietly, "will you please do me a favor? Don't ask Barbara to tell you what happened that has worried her. It was nothing but an unfortunate mistake, and will all blow over in the morning."

"Very well, Ruth," agreed Mollie. "I won't ask. But I am not a baby, and I am very sure it would be better if I were told."

Thus poor Bab had no one in whom to confide, and had to bear her ugly secret all alone.

Ruth kissed her good night, saying: "Cheer up, silly girl, and sleep late as you can in the morning. You know, it's to be the last day of our tennis practice, and you are going to beat me tomorrow!"

Ruth tiptoed over to Mollie, who was undressing in silence. "Mistress Mollie," she said, "forgive me; do, please, like a dear. Talking about horrid things only makes them *horrider!*"

Ruth, in the depths of her heart, thought that Barbara had been most unwise in her hinted accusation of Harry Townsend. For Bab's sake she thought it best for everyone to forget what had happened. It was a fault in Ruth's nature that she loved only pleasant things, and would often give up, even when she knew she was right, in order not to make trouble.

The next morning a Barbara of heavy eyes and white cheeks joined the players on the tennis court.

Plainly Harry had confided what had happened to Gladys, for she did not speak to Bab as she came up to her, but tossed her head and bit her lips. Gladys said nothing, however, for Harry had made her promise she would not breathe what he had told her.

As for Mr. Townsend, he treated Barbara with cold politeness. But Barbara was beginning to have her eyes opened. "If I am right about him," she thought to herself, "then I shall have to be very careful. I believe he is more clever than any of us dream!"

It was Hugh whose manner was most constrained. He could not forgive the scene of the night before, in which he had been forced to take an unwilling part. Not until Ruth called him over to her, and gave him a lecture, did he beg Bab's pardon, and ask that they all forget the experience of the night before.

"Come on!" he called, cheerily, to the group of tennis players. "It's do or die to-day—the last test day for us. It will show us who is to represent our crowd at the tournament. The girl and the fellow who can beat all the rest of us stand a good chance of winning the silver cup. Mrs. Cartwright says she has been closely following the game of the star players and she thinks we have them beaten to a finish. Come on, Ruth, let's show 'em that we're out for blood!"

Swish! Barbara's ball flew over the net and curved toward the ground at Hugh's left. Not too swiftly for that young gentleman; while Ruth's heart gave a jump of apprehension, Hugh made a left-hand swing with his racquet and sent the ball whizzing back.

"Fifteen!" Ralph called out, in a bored tone. He had failed in his return.

The battle raged all morning.

Grace and Donald Cartwright, Gladys and Mr. Townsend were soon out of the running. When they had finished they sank gratefully on the ground, to watch the others play.

The field was thus left to Barbara and Ralph, to Ruth and Hugh. The sets stood even, and two more games would decide.

A small crowd of visitors stood around the court. Mrs. Cartwright, having finished her own game, came over to look on. Miss Sallie was trying to be impartial, but she was really deeply interested in Ruth's success. Mrs. Erwin, Mrs. Post, the governor, all their friends, were lined up to behold the battle.

A subdued discussion of the lost emeralds had

been going on at the Casino all morning. After a thorough search of every inch of Mrs. Erwin's house and grounds, there was still no sign of the jewels; but Governor Post and Mrs. Erwin had made every effort to have the scandal of the necklace hushed up. They had seen the Newport detectives, and had telegraphed to New York for two experts to be sent down to handle the case. In the meantime they had been advised not to talk.

Now the only upright person, who could have given them any information had, for just a little while, forgotten all about it. Whatever Barbara did she did with her whole heart. Today she played tennis.

"Ralph," Hugh called, "remember, now, it's two straight games to finish the way we stand!"

There was no more conversation. Even the watchers held their breath. The referee sat on the ground, rapidly calling out the score—"forty—thirty—deuce!"

"Is this game to go on forever?" Miss Sallie inquired, plaintively. "My girls will be wholly worn out."

"Advantage in!" shouted the referee.

Ralph sprang forward for his ball; his foot slipped. Barbara, who had been expecting him to return it, was not ready.

"Game!"

Ruth and Hugh shook hands with each other. But Hugh called over: "Say, Ralph, was this game all right? You turned your ankle, didn't you?"

"Surely I did," said Ralph. "I was an idiot, but it

is your game just the same. I'll make it up next time, Barbara—see if I don't!"

"My dear Ruth," said Miss Sallie, "I cannot permit it. You will be exhausted."

"Here, Barbara," said Mollie, "do try to get your breath, and let me fix up your hair."

"No prinking!" Ralph called out. "This is business, ladies!"

The good old Casino courts never saw a finer tennis battle. Ralph and Bab played as though they had forgotten their talk in the woods that day when they had tea at Mrs. Duffy's. Ruth and Hugh were foeman worthy of their best steel.

The game stood forty-all, and it was Bab's serve. Bab's serves were what made her tennis remarkable. They were as swift and straight and true as a boy's.

Hugh stood ready waiting. Barbara caught a look in Ruth's face, on the other side of the net. Her big blue eyes, frank and clear as a baby's, were glowing with interest, with hope, with ambition! Like a flash the thought of all Ruth had done for them came into Bab's mind. Did it weaken the force of her drive? Or was it because her mind was distracted? The ball fell just inside the net on her own side.

"Try again, partner mine!" shouted Ralph, "show 'em what you're made of!"

This time Barbara was plainly nervous. She felt that nearly all the friends around them wanted Ruth to win. They would be delighted, of course, with her success and kind to her, but open-hearted and open-handed Ruth was the favorite with them all; at least, Bab thought so.

With returning courage, Bab hit her last ball a hard blow. It rose high in the air! Hugh sprang on his tip-toes to receive it and gave a mighty shout. The ball had fallen outside the line.

Ralph and Barbara were the first to congratulate the victors. Barbara cleared the net with a bound, forgetting both her age and her audience.

"There, Ruth, you and Hugh are the best players that ever happened!" Barbara spoke with a glowing face. Then she turned to Ralph: "I lost the game for you," she said. "I am so sorry."

"Oh, no, you didn't, my lady," said Ralph. "I lost the game before this one, so we're even."

An admiring circle had formed around Ruth and Hugh. "Your father will be delighted, I know, child," said Miss Sallie.

"I haven't won the cup yet, Auntie," protested Ruth.

"But you must, child," said Mrs. Cartwright, smiling. "I am betting on you and Hugh in the tournament, and you mustn't make me lose my box of candy."

"Barbara," said Ralph, shyly, as they walked off toward home a little later, "I don't like to ask you, but did you mean to miss those last serves?"

Barbara shook her head. "No," she said, "I don't think I meant to. I don't know. But they were the best players, weren't they, Ralph?"

"Certainly," Ralph answered.

CHAPTER XV
·············
Ruth in Danger

Hugh, looking much embarrassed, came up early next morning to see Ruth.

"I have an invitation to deliver to you, Ruth, but I am rather ashamed to do it, for I am afraid you will be angry. Mother told me to come over and ask Miss Stuart and yourself and the girls—except Barbara—to come out with us for the day on the yacht."

"Why, Hugh Post!" cried Ruth. "What do you mean?"

"Well, it's like this," Hugh said, desperately; "mother told me to explain to you exactly how things stand, so you will not think her rude. You see, mother is visiting Mrs. Erwin, and of course Mrs. Erwin, Gladys, and her devoted Harry Townsend have to go along on the yacht with us. Well, Gladys told mother that neither she nor Mr. Townsend could go if Barbara went. Gladys would not tell mother why, and, as you told me to keep that scene in the conservatory a secret, I didn't know what it was wisest for me to do."

"Thank you," Ruth answered; "but tell your mother that none of us can accept."

"O Ruth!" exclaimed Hugh. "I am fearfully disappointed, and mother I know will be angry."

"I am afraid I don't care, Hugh," was Ruth's reply. "I don't like your mother's inviting any of us, if she had to leave Bab out."

As Hugh turned to leave the front porch, where he had found Ruth alone, she called after him: "Wait a minute, please. I don't know what to tell Aunt Sallie. Your mother will be sure to speak to her of her invitation, and Auntie will think I should have let her refuse for herself. Oh, I know!"

Ruth's face cleared. "I will go tell Aunt Sallie that she and Grace and Mollie are asked. I'll stay with my dear Bab," she finished a little defiantly. "If I am also left out of the party, no one will think anything of it."

"Oh, I say, Ruth," Hugh urged, "please come."

"Sorry," she said, shaking her head decidedly.

"I expect you're right," Hugh replied.

Miss Sallie, Mollie and Grace accepted Mrs. Post's invitation with pleasure. As Mrs. Post's yacht was small, they did not think it strange that the other two girls were left out.

How angry Mollie would have been, had she guessed the truth. Not a step would she have gone. As it was, she begged Barbara to go in her place.

But Bab was too clever. She understood what had happened, and was glad to be left out of the party. She put her arm around Ruth's waist, whispering coaxingly: "Do go along with the others, old story-teller. You know you were asked."

Ruth shook her head decidedly. "Not on your life," she slangily retorted. Fortunately, Miss Sallie did not hear her.

"What shall we do this afternoon, Bab?" inquired Ruth after luncheon. "Suppose you and I go for a long walk?"

"Don't think I am a lazy good-for-nothing, Ruth," Barbara begged, "but I have a little headache, and I must write to mother. Mollie and I have been neglecting her shamefully of late. I haven't even written her about the wonderful ball."

"Are you going to tell her what happened, Bab?" Ruth inquired.

"I suppose so," sighed Bab. She was half inclined to discuss the unfortunate affair with Ruth, but changed her mind.

"Well, Bab," Ruth declared, "I shall go for the walk 'all by my lonesomes.' I'll be back in time for dinner. The others are to dine on the yacht, so we need not look for them until bedtime. I think I'll take the cliff walk, for the sea is so splendid to-day."

Left alone, Barbara got out her writing materials and sat down by the window, but she did not begin to write.

"I wonder," she asked herself, "why we have been mixed up in burglaries ever since Ruth began talking about our trip to Newport? First, our poor little twenty-dollar gold-pieces disappear; then we have that dreadful robber at New Haven. Now Mrs. Post's emerald necklace is stolen! It could not all have been Mr. Townsend!" Barbara sat with her hands clenched.

"If it is true," she went on, "and I saw the necklace disappear with my own eyes, then we have another Raffles to deal with. Mr. Raffles, the second! I believe I am the only person that suspects him. Well, Mr. Harry Townsend!" Barbara's red lips tightened, "you are successful now, but we shall see whose wits are better, yours or mine!"

Barbara's face turned a deep crimson. "I understood. He wanted to suggest I was the thief. Only he didn't dare to accuse me openly the other night. I won't tell mother," Barbara at last decided. "I'll just watch—and wait!"

Barbara wrote her mother a long, happy letter, without a hint of the troubles she began to feel closing in on her. Then she straightened her own and Mollie's bureau drawers and arranged their clothes in the two closets. Still Ruth did not come.

Twice Barbara went into her room. It was half past five—six—Mrs. Ewing's early dinner was served at half after six.

"Mrs. Ewing," Barbara said, knocking timidly at her door. "Have you seen anything of Ruth? She has been gone such a long time that I am worried about her."

But Mrs. Ewing knew nothing of her.

"I believe I'll go to meet her," said Barbara, "and hurry her along. She must be on her way home." Ralph was on the yacht with Hugh, or Barbara would have asked him to accompany her.

For the first half mile along the cliff walk Barbara strolled slowly, expecting every moment to see Ruth hurrying along. As the walk dipped down into hollows and rose again in the high places, it was difficult to see any distance ahead.

The walk was entirely deserted, and Bab's heart commenced to beat faster as the darkness began to gather.

"I suppose," thought Barbara, "Ruth has gone somewhere to make a visit, and has stayed late without thinking. She's probably at home, now, waiting for me, so I'll get the scolding from Mrs. Ewing for being late to dinner. I believe I'll go on back home." Barbara actually turned and started in the opposite direction.

Something within her seemed to call: "Bab! Bab!" The voice was so urgent she was frightened. "Ruth needs you," it seemed to say.

Bab began calling aloud, "Ruth! Ruth!" Her voice sounded high and shrill in her own ears; but only the echo answered her, and the noise of the waves pounding against the shore. She could see the distant lights in the houses along the way, but Barbara dared not stop to ask for help while that inner voice urged her on.

Barbara was running, now, along the narrow, difficult path. "O Ruth, dear Ruth!" she cried. "Why don't you answer me? Are you anywhere, needing me?" She heard a low sound and stopped. Nothing but her own imagination! There were always queer noises along the cliff shore, where the water swirled into little eddies and gurgled out again.

Barbara waited. She heard nothing more, so she plunged on. Suddenly she drew back with a gasp of horror. Part of the cliff walk had disappeared! Where a bridge of stone had spanned a narrow chasm there was a terrible, yawning hole. Jutting out their vicious arms were rocks, rocks, forming a sheer drop of seventy feet to the beach below.

Involuntarily, Barbara had flung herself down on her hands and knees to keep from falling over into the abyss.

"Ruth couldn't have," she thought. "No, no!" But hark! Was that again the low moaning sound of the waters? Barbara lay flat on the rocks, stretching her head over the embankment. There, in a cleft between two great rocks, fifteen feet below her, a dark object hung!

"Ruth! Ruth!" Bab called, her voice coming from her throat in a hoarse cry. Again she heard the faint moan. This time she knew the sound. It was Ruth! What could she do? Run for help? Any second, Bab realized, Ruth's strength might fail, and she would let go her grasp. Barbara could not bear to think of the horrible end.

As far as she could see, Ruth's feet rested on a narrow ledge of rock, while she clung with her hands to a cliff that jutted out overhead. "Ruth! Ruth!" Barbara called again, but this time her voice was clear and strong. "It is Bab! Do you understand? Hold on a little longer. I am coming."

Swiftly a prayer came into Barbara's mind: "Lord, show me the way." Yet even while she prayed she acted. "Help, help!" Bab called out.

She tore off the long woolen shawl which she had wrapped round her when she came out to seek Ruth. With hands that seemed to gain a superhuman strength Bab tore it into three, four strips. She dared not make the strips narrower for fear they would not hold. Then she took off her skirt of light wool and wrenched it into broad bands. How, Barbara never knew. She felt that the power was given her.

Growing out from a rock between Bab and the moaning figure on the cliff below was a small tree, its roots deeply imbedded in the hard soil. Ruth had evidently reached out to grasp this tree as the cliff bridge gave way beneath her feet; but, missing it, her feet had touched a ledge of rock and she had flung out her arms and clasped the stone above her. How much longer would her failing strength serve her?

Bab again lay down and measured the length of her queer rope. She found that by reaching the tree she could tie the rope to it and it would then be long enough to extend to Ruth. Removing her shoes, Barbara slowly, and with infinite caution, crawled down the jagged rocks, clinging with her hands and toes. Finally she arrived at the tree, and fastened her rope securely around it, only to find it dangled just above Ruth's head. Yet what was

Barbara Lay Flat on the Rocks.
[illustration from the 1910 edition]

the use? If Ruth for an instant let go the rock to which she clung her feet would slip from the ledge, and Bab's poor woolen strings could never hold her.

But Barbara understood this. She was face to face with the great moment of her life, and, though she was only a simple country girl, neither her brains nor her strength failed her.

Did she stop at the tree after the rope was tied? No! Still clinging, sliding, her hands bruised and bleeding, Barbara was making her way to where Ruth hung. Bab had said truly that she could climb. Never had a girl a better opportunity to prove her boast! There were moments when she believed she could not go on. Then the thought of Ruth renewed her courage.

Just above Ruth's head, on the left side of her, was a great boulder with a curved, smooth surface. It was to this rock Bab made her way. She was so close to Ruth now that she could lean over and touch her. "Courage, dear," she whispered, and she thought she saw Ruth's pale lips smile. She had not fainted; for this, Barbara was grateful.

When Barbara was a little girl her mother had been ashamed of her tomboy ways; but she had given in, with a gentle sigh, when Bab grew and flourished by playing boys' games, by learning various boyish arts; among them was the knack of tying a sailor knot.

Edging closer and closer to Ruth she managed to reach out and catch hold of the rope she had fastened to the tree. With one hand on her own rock, with the other she drew the cord about Ruth, fastening it firmly under her arms. The rope was not strong enough to draw Ruth up to safety, but it would steady her should her hands give way.

Somehow, in some way, Barbara must get further help.

Now that her first duty was over, she began to call loudly: "Help, help!" Her shouts roused Ruth, who joined feebly in the cry. No sound answered them. Only the seagulls swept over them, uttering their hoarse call.

Barbara felt her own strength going. She tried to crawl up the slippery rock again, but her power was gone. She, too, felt herself—slipping, slipping! With one wild cry she caught at her rock, and all was still!

CHAPTER XVI
· · · · · · · · · · · · · ·
Help Arrives

Mr. Cartwright was dining alone on his Japanese veranda, as his wife was with the yachting party, and was not expected to dinner.

Jones, the butler, came in softly, placing the soup in front of his master. As he put down the plate his hand shook. Surely he heard a cry!

At the same moment Mr. Cartwright started up. "Jones, what was that?" They both stood still. There was no further sound.

"Must 'ave been children playing, sir," suggested Jones, and Mr. Cartwright continued his dinner.

"Help, help!" The sound came from afar off, loud and shrill. This time there was no mistake.

"Coming!" Mr. Cartwright shouted. "Coming!" As he ran across the lawn, closely followed by Jones, he snatched a heavy coil of rope left by the workmen who had been swinging hammocks and arranging for Mrs. Cartwright's outdoor bazaar.

"Call again, if you can," Mr. Cartwright yelled. Faintly,

a voice seemed to come up out of the earth. "Help, help! Oh, please!"

Mr. Cartwright caught the direction of the voice, and ran along the cliffs. In a moment he espied the fallen bridge and guessed what had happened; then he and Jones saw the two girls in their perilous position.

Leaning over, he called: "Can you hear me?"

Bab answered, "Yes."

"Then keep still," shouted Mr. Cartwright, "and I'll have you up here in a moment."

Quickly he knotted the rope around Jones's waist; then, some yards farther on, he tied it round his own. "Go back," he said to his butler, "and lie down." Jones was large and heavy; Mr. Cartwright was a tall man, thin, but strong.

Slowly he lowered himself to the tree where Bab had tied her poor rope, and flung an improvised lasso over to Bab. "Not me," said Barbara, forgetting her grammar. "Ruth first."

"Can she climb with the help of the rope?" asked their rescuer.

Ruth had not spoken, but she opened her eyes, gave a shudder and fainted.

Like a flash Bab had thrown the lasso over her shoulders, and Ruth hung swaying in the air! Fortunately her feet were still on the ledge of the rock. Mr. Cartwright caught his rope round the tree, at the same time calling to Jones, "Throw me another coil!" He then clambered down and half carried, half dragged the fainting Ruth to the top of the cliff.

Once above, he dropped his burden, and again flung the lasso over the edge of the rocks to Barbara, who, crawling and being pulled by turns, came up in safety. When she had reached the top, and stood by the side of the fainting Ruth, Bab's courage deserted her, and she burst into tears.

"Get the young ladies to the house at once," ordered Mr. Cartwright, far more frightened than he had been while playing rescuer.

How fared the yachting party? They did not have a good day. Hugh was in a bad humor because Ruth had not come; Ralph missed Barbara, and, try as they might to avoid it, the conversation would drift back to the lost emeralds.

"I shall never understand it," said Mrs. Erwin to Aunt Sallie, in subdued tones. "The detectives say they have made a thorough search of my servants' quarters, have watched their movements ever since the night of the theft, and they can find none of them of whom they are even suspicious. They do say"—this time Mrs. Erwin dropped her voice to a whisper, for the woman who was with Mrs. Post at the time of the robbery was approaching them—"they say that the burglar was probably—one of the guests!"

This woman, who had worn a gold-colored brocade, was an American, who had married a Frenchman, but her husband was supposed to have been dead several years. She had come to Newport, this season, with letters of introduction, and was already very popular.

"Do you know," she inquired, "where Miss Le Baron and Mr. Townsend are? No one has seen them recently."

"Oh," laughed Mrs. Erwin, "we leave those two young people alone. I believe they have an affair of their own. Have you known Mr. Townsend before this meeting?"

"Oh, no," replied the woman, in a curious tone; "at least, I have met him once or twice. I can't say I know him."

"Ladies," Governor Post said, coming up to them, "I believe I will cheat you of part of your sail today. There are ugly clouds gathering, and I think it better to put into harbor. We can go ashore, or not, as we feel inclined."

As the yacht neared the shore, Miss Sallie grew restless. It was the first time since the beginning of their trip that she had been separated from any of her girls. As soon as dinner was over she begged Governor Post to put herself, Grace and Mollie ashore. Immediately the rest of the party agreed to disembark with her.

Ralph and the two girls followed Aunt Sallie home. For once, she hurried on before them, urged by a kind of foreboding.

She found Mrs. Ewing, white and frightened, walking up and down in front of her gate. Mr. Ewing and the maids had left the house, half an hour before, to search for the lost girls.

Thoughtlessly Mrs. Ewing rushed up to Miss Stuart. "Have Ruth and Barbara joined you?" she asked.

"Why, no," replied the two girls in amazement. Ralph stared in surprise; but Miss Sallie spoke firmly. "Tell me, at once, what has happened." In the midst of real danger Miss Stuart was a different woman, as Mr. Stuart well knew when he allowed her to chaperon the automobile girls.

Mrs. Ewing had nothing to tell. All she knew was that the girls had gone out for a long walk, and, at eight o'clock, had not come back.

"Come with me, Ralph," Miss Sallie demanded. Grace and Mollie followed them.

"Don't be frightened, Mollie," Grace begged, trying to talk cheerfully, though she was trembling violently. "Rely upon Ruth and Bab to get safely out of a scrape."

Just as they reached the end of the street that turned into the cliff walk, Miss Sallie espied a servant of the Cartwrights running in their direction. "Stop him!" she commanded Ralph.

"Sure, mum, I am to tell you," the gardener's boy said, "the young ladies was not killed."

"Not killed!" the girls cried, in horror. Ralph took hold of Mollie's hand.

"That is what I was to say, mum," said the boy, evidently much excited. "They is not much hurt and will be home soon."

"Take me to them, at once," ordered Miss Sallie,

asking no further questions. The gardener's boy led the way.

When the party arrived, Mrs. Cartwright, still in her yachting suit, ran out to meet them. Ruth came to the door, walking a little stiffly. Barbara followed her, and straightway begged Mollie not to cry.

"It's all over, silly little Mollie," she whispered, "and neither Ruth nor I am hurt. We are just a little scratched, and very dirty, and we want to go to bed."

"Mr. Cartwright has already had the doctor in to see us, Auntie," said Ruth. "He is in the drawing room now. We have no broken bones or strains, though my shoulders ache rather badly."

Mollie and Grace were both crying, just because there was nothing, now, for them to cry about.

Miss Sallie made Ruth sit down again, as her niece was almost too weak to stand. After listening in silence to Ruth's story, Aunt Sallie held out her hand to Mr. Cartwright. "My brother and I can never thank you, and I shall not attempt it. Ruth means all our world." Then she turned to Barbara, and gathered her in her arms. "My child," she said, "you are the bravest girl I ever knew." Miss Stuart choked, and could say no more.

"Do you remember, Bab," asked Mollie, when Barbara was safe in her own bed, "how once you said you would one day repay Ruth and Mr. Stuart for their kindness to us? Well, I think, and I know they will think, that you have kept your promise. Yes; I'm going to let her go to sleep, Miss Sallie," Mollie called back, in answer to Miss Stuart's remonstrance.

Ruth and Barbara were utterly worn out, and had been put into warm baths and rubbed down with alcohol. "I am not even going to give two such sensible girls doses of aromatic spirits of ammonia," declared the doctor, who had driven over from Mrs. Cartwright's with them and had seen the girls safely in bed. "They will be all right in a day or two," he assured Miss Sallie, "as soon as they get over the nervous shock."

It took six telegrams to Mr. Stuart and Mrs. Thurston to persuade them the girls were unhurt and able to remain in Newport.

CHAPTER XVII

The Fortune-Tellers

"My dears," said Mrs. Cartwright, two days after the accident, coming into the sitting-room, where Ruth and Bab were idling, "I suppose you know that you are the heroines of Newport. No one is talking about anything but your accident. You have almost put the jewel robbery out of our minds. How do you feel this morning?"

"Oh, as fit as anything," smiled Ruth, though she still looked a little pale. "I have just written a long letter to father, to assure him that I shall be well enough to play in the tournament next week."

"That is fine," declared Mrs. Cartwright. "And you, Bab?"

"There never was much the matter with me," Bab answered.

"Then you are just the girls I am looking for," said Mrs. Cartwright, clapping her hands. "You know, I asked you, Bab, to play gypsy fortune-teller at my bazaar; now I want to ask Ruth to join you. Everyone thinks you are both laid up from your accident, and no one will suspect who you are. The plans for the bazaar are going splendidly. I think I shall make lots of money for my poor sailors. I shall have it as simple and attractive as I can—a real country fair, with booths and lemonade stands. I am going to give these jaded Newport people a taste of the simple life. Do say you will help me."

Both girls shook their heads. "We do not know how to tell fortunes," they protested.

"Oh, it's only fun," argued Mrs. Cartwright. "You can make up any foolishness you like as you go along. I'll show you how to run the cards, as they call it. Has either of you ever seen anyone do it?"

Bab confessed she had watched "Granny Ann." Suddenly she left her chair, and came hobbling over to Mrs. Cartwright, saying, in Granny Ann's own high-pitched, whining voice: "Lovely lady, would you know the future, grave or gay, cross my hand with a silver piece and list to what I say."

Gravely, Mrs. Cartwright extracted a dollar from her silver purse, and made the gypsy sign on Bab's out-stretched hand. Barbara immediately told her such a nonsensical fortune, in a perfectly grave voice, that she and Ruth both screamed with laughter.

"You'll do, Bab," said Mrs. Cartwright. "Won't you join her, Ruth?"

"Well," said Ruth, "I never desert Mrs. Micawber these days, or, to put it plainly, Miss Bab Thurston. So I'm game."

"Thursday, then, remember, and this is Tuesday,"

said Mrs. Cartwright. "I am the busiest woman in Newport, so I must run away now. You should see my house and lawn. They are full of workmen. The fair is to begin promptly at four, and will last until midnight. We shall have dancing on the lawn, but I want you girls and a few friends to come into the house after supper. When you finish playing fortune-tellers you can slip up to my room and dress. Nobody must guess, when you come down, that you have not just arrived. Now, I positively must be off. Tell Mollie and Grace I am depending on them to act as waitresses. Gladys isn't willing to help. She wants all her time for Harry Townsend."

"Ruth," said Aunt Sallie, the afternoon of the bazaar, "I really cannot permit you to go anywhere, looking as you do, even if you are wearing a disguise. You are too horrible!"

"Come and see Barbara," Grace called from the next room. "I am sure she must look worse. Why," she asked, laughing, "do you and Ruth want to disguise yourselves as such dreadful-looking gypsies. You might just as easily have arranged to look like young and charming ones."

"Oh, no," said Bab. "We want to look like the real thing, not like stage gypsies." Barbara had arranged to appear as much like "Granny Ann" as she possibly could. A red and yellow handkerchief was bound around her head almost to her eyebrows, her face was stained to a deep brown, with lines and heavy seams drawn over it; even her hands were made up to look old and weather beaten.

"Remember, you have never seen nor heard of these extraordinary fortune-tellers before," warned Ruth. "And don't forget, Barbara and Ruth are at home at Mrs. Ewing's, but they may feel well enough to come to the fair in the evening." Ruth caught Bab's arm, and together they made a low curtsey.

"Beautiful ones," Ruth went on, pointing to Miss Sallie, who was looking handsome in a gown of pale gray crêpe, with a violet hat and sunshade, and to Mollie and Grace, who were dressed like Swiss peasant girls, "your fortunes I would like to tell before you go to the Fair. Easy it is for my wise eyes to perceive that you will be the belles and beauties of the entertainment. Now, farewell!"

The "gypsies" were to drive over early to Mrs. Cartwright's in a closed carriage. Ralph was to take Miss Sallie, Grace and Mollie in the motor car later on.

"Granny Ann" and "old Meg" slipped inside the gypsy tent before any of the guests had arrived at the bazaar. They had gazed in wonder at Mrs. Cartwright's beautiful lawn, changed to look like a country fair. It was hung with bunting and flags, and had small tables and chairs under the trees; also a May-pole strung with long streamers of different colored ribbons. Mrs. Cartwright had planned a May-pole dance as one of the chief features of the afternoon, and Mollie and Grace were both to take part.

For the gypsies, life was a serious matter. The tent was divided by a red curtain; on a low wooden table burned a round iron pot filled with charcoal and curious odorous herbs; a pack of dirty cards lay near it. "The cards must be dirty," argued Ruth, "or no one would believe we were the real thing in gypsies." Two rough stools stood by the table, and the only daylight shone through the tent flap. On the other side of the curtain, Mrs. Cartwright had been kinder to her gypsies. Here were a wicker couch and big chairs, where they could rest and talk; also a table for refreshments, "for," laughed Mrs. Cartwright, as she left the tent to welcome her first guests, "I have always heard that gypsies are a particularly hungry race of people."

Mrs. Cartwright's fair was a huge success. The most fashionable "set" in Newport were present, entering into the spirit of the occasion with great zest.

Gladys and Harry Townsend were seen everywhere together; but to-day there was often a third person with them, the Countess Bertouche, the woman of the gold-colored brocade, but lately introduced in Newport society.

"I believe Gladys is engaged to Harry Townsend," whispered Grace to Mollie, when she had observed Harry bending over Miss Le Baron and talking to her in a more devoted manner than usual.

"Well," retorted pretty Mollie, with a toss of her head, "I am sure I do not envy either one of them."

All afternoon the gypsy tent had been flooded with visitors. Barbara and Ruth had the time of their lives. No one recognized the two automobile girls in the aged crones who mumbled and told strange fortunes in hoarse tones.

It was growing late, and the gypsy tent was for the time deserted. Ruth was resting on the couch in the back of the tent, while Bab sat near her, talking over their experiences of the afternoon.

Suddenly the tent flap opened, and Grace and Mollie rushed in. Before either of them spoke, they turned and fastened the flap down again securely, so no one could enter without their knowing it.

"What's the matter?" asked Ruth and Bab at once, for it was plain to see their visitors were greatly excited.

Grace and Mollie started talking together. "Mrs. Cartwright's diamond butterfly——" then they both stopped. "Are you sure no one can hear? Mollie, you tell," finished Grace.

"The butterfly has gone, vanished right off Mrs. Cartwright's frock, this afternoon, while she was talking to her visitors. You know, she changed the ornament she wore in her hair into a brooch. She showed it to me early this afternoon, when I first came, and now—it is gone! I tell you, girls, there's a thief among these Newport people. I think it, and so does Mrs. Cartwright, and ever so many others. Promise you'll never tell," went on Mollie, "but there are two detectives here watching all the guests! I'd like to find the thief myself. I'd know Mrs. Cartwright's butterfly anywhere."

There were noises at the tent door.

Barbara heard Gladys's high, querulous voice, saying, coquettishly: "I don't want my fortune told, Harry. I would much rather you told it to me any way." But Mr. Townsend insisted.

"Fly, girls—do, please! They are coming in!" said Barbara. "No; you can't get out, but you must stay perfectly still behind this curtain, and not breathe a single word."

It was almost entirely dark in the gypsy tent, the only light coming from the burning pot of fire on the table. Barbara stooped low, when she opened the door to allow Harry, Gladys and the Countess Bertouche to come in.

"It groweth late," Bab began, croakingly. "Evil may come. No good fortunes fall between dusk and darkness. Beware!"

Gladys shuddered. "Let's not go in," she urged.

But Harry Townsend only laughed. "Don't let the old hag frighten you," he retorted, lightly. "Here," he turned to the gypsy and spoke in a voice no one of the girls had ever heard him use, "here, you old swindler, speak out! What kind of fate do you read for me in the stars?"

Barbara picked up the pack of dirty cards, and began to shuffle them slowly. An idea was revolving in her head. Dared she do it? But Barbara was a girl who was not easily daunted.

After a minute of silence she shook her head. "What I see I dare not reveal," she whined. "All black, dark, dark mystery!"

"Oh, stuff!" jeered Mr. Townsend. "Don't try that dodge on me. Tell what you know."

Barbara flung down the cards and blew three puffs into the smouldering pot of fire. Ashes and tiny flames shot up from it. She started back, then pointing a finger, she hissed: "Something is moving toward you, curving and coiling and twisting round you. Mercy!" she cried. "It is a green snake, and its fangs have struck into your soul!"

Harry Townsend's face grew livid. In a moment the look of youth vanished from his face, his lips turned blue, and his eyes narrowed to two fine points.

The Countess Bertouche came forward. "Harry," she said, "come away. You forget yourself. Don't listen to such nonsense."

"Harry!" thought Gladys to herself, angrily. "She certainly presumes on a short acquaintance! Harry, indeed!"

But Barbara had not finished.

"Stay!" she said, holding up a warning finger. "Another messenger appears. It is a beautiful, bright thing, sparkling and darting toward you. Why," she added, quickly, "it is lighting on your coat. It has flown inside—a beautiful butterfly, born of summer time and

Harry Townsend's Face Grew Livid.
[illustration from the 1910 edition]

flowers. Or"—this time Barbara leaned over and whispered in his ear—"or it may be made of diamonds and come from a jeweler's shop."

For an instant, Harry Townsend's hand flew to his vest pocket. He rose, saying quietly to his companions: "Come away from here. Did you ever see such a stupid old fraud? A snake and a butterfly—a curious fortune indeed!"

CHAPTER XVIII

A Word to the Wise

Barbara's suspicion was now a certainty. Another person might not have been much wiser from Harry Townsend's behavior during the telling of his fortune. But Barbara's eyes were keen. The thief the detectives were seeking, the "Raffles" who was bowing and smiling his way through Newport society was none other than "Harry Townsend." How to prove it? That was another matter.

"Bab," said the other girls, appearing on her side of the tent, "what a string of nonsense you did put off on poor Harry Townsend. What on earth made you tell him about a butterfly and a snake? I suppose you had butterfly on the brain, since we had just told you of the robbery."

"That is true," assented Bab.

"Ruth!" Barbara turned to her quickly. "I am tired of my job. I want to quit this fortune-telling business at once. Let's desert and go up to Mrs. Cartwright's room and change our clothes. Do hurry!" she urged, a little impatiently.

"Oh, all right, Bab," Ruth agreed. She stared at Barbara curiously. What had come over her friend? Harry Townsend always seemed to have such a strange effect upon her.

Barbara was thinking. How could she find the detectives, to tell them of her suspicions, while Harry Townsend still had in his pocket the jewel he had stolen?

"I want to ask you something, Mollie," Bab announced, as the girls started for the house. "You'll excuse a family secret, won't you?" she asked of Grace and Ruth. "Mollie," Bab whispered, "don't speak out loud. Do you think you can discover who the two detectives are, and let me know as soon as I come downstairs? Don't ask questions, please; only, I must know."

Mollie shut her lips close together. "Yes, I'll find out for you," she promised.

Half an hour later, as the guests were being served with supper under the trees, Ruth and Barbara made their appearance.

"We just couldn't keep away any longer," they explained to their friends. "Oh, yes, we are feeling perfectly well again."

Barbara called Mrs. Cartwright aside for a minute. "Is it true," she asked, "that your diamond butterfly has disappeared?"

Mrs. Cartwright's face clouded. "Yes," she replied. "It has gone within the last hour or so. I had it fastened here on my dress with a long pin. If it was stolen by a guest, which I am coming to believe, then it was not such a difficult theft. I have been leaning over, laughing and talking, and any light-fingered—woman—or man— could easily have taken it out of my dress."

Mrs. Cartwright shivered and turned pale, as she looked at the gay parties of people out on her lawn. "Isn't it dreadful," she said, plaintively, "to think that there may be a thief right over there among all my friends! But run along, now, child, and enjoy yourself. You and Ruth were the success of the afternoon. Everyone has asked me where I found my clever gypsies."

Barbara wandered off alone. Before she had gone more than a few steps, Ralph Ewing joined her. "Please don't come with me, Ralph," she begged. "I want to find Mollie."

"Well, why should that prevent my coming along, too?" Ralph asked. "I'd like to find Mollie myself. She hasn't paid the slightest attention to me all afternoon."

"I don't want to be horrid, Ralph," Barbara protested, nervously, "but please let me find her by myself."

"Oh, certainly," assented Ralph, walking quickly away.

Over by one of the lemonade stands that had been deserted at supper time Bab found Mollie.

"Bab," she said, pulling her sister to one side, "do you see that tall, blond man, with the little, curly mustache? He is one of the detectives. I can't find out where the other one is."

A little later Ralph Ewing, who was still strolling around by himself, felt his face flush, partly with wounded pride, partly with anger. Barbara was not talking to Mollie. She was standing some distance off from the other guests, having an earnest conversation with a man whom Ralph knew to be a stranger in Newport.

Ralph was too proud to linger near them, since Bab had said so plainly she wanted none of his society. If he could have heard what she was saying he would have been even more horrified.

"Yes," Barbara promised, "if you will come somewhere near us, when we are all together, this evening, I will give you a signal to show you the man I mean. His name is Townsend. He looks very young, is slender and is of medium height. Suppose, when you see us, I bow my head slowly in the direction of the man I mean? If you understand me, you can return my bow. Can you search him before he leaves the grounds?"

"No, miss." The detective shook his head. "It would be impossible. He hasn't the jewel on him now. If he's the man we think he is, he is too smooth for that. He must have a confederate. If we search him here, and find no proof of his guilt, he will know all about us and our suspicions. Can't you see, then, he would just clear out and leave us here to whistle for our pains?"

"Yes, I see," said Bab.

"Thank you, miss, for telling us," the detective continued. "I must say that emerald story sounds like the real thing. You've only guessed about the butterfly theft;

but I think you've guessed right. Now we must go easy. If there is a Raffles, here in Newport, he is out for more plunder. He'll make another bold attempt, and that will be our chance."

"Well, I must go on back now to my friends," murmured Barbara, uneasily. It seemed strange to be taken into confidence by the detective, as though she were in the same line of business. "I suppose you and the other detective can manage, now, to secure the thief. I would rather not have anything more to do with the matter." Barbara gave a little shiver of repulsion.

"Oh, now, young lady," protested the detective, "you mustn't go back on us, just as the game commences. To catch a society thief we must have help from the inside. The best detective in the service can't get on without it."

"Where have you been, Bab?" inquired Miss Sallie, anxiously, when Barbara joined her friends a few minutes later. "I was beginning to get uneasy about you. Mrs. Cartwright wants us to come into the house for an informal dance. Do you feel well enough to go? I don't think you look very well, child."

Harry Townsend and Gladys came up at this minute. Harry had promised to take Miss Stuart indoors to watch the dancing. There was a curious, restless look in the man's eyes, but his manners were as charming as ever.

This was Barbara's chance. She lagged behind the others, and bowed her head slowly in the direction of Miss Sallie's escort. A strange, blond man, with a curly light mustache, standing some distance off, returned her bow.

All evening Ralph did not come near Barbara. He devoted himself to Grace, who was wise enough to guess that Bab and Ralph must have had a quarrel. But Barbara did not understand. Not having realized that Ralph had felt snubbed when she dismissed him a little while before, she supposed he had grown tired of her.

To tell the truth, Barbara was dull. All the merry, sparkling fun had gone out of her for this one evening. Whether she danced, or talked or rested quietly, she saw Harry Townsend's face as it had looked at her for a single minute in the gypsy tent. "I am not a coward," thought Barbara, "but I shall have to be careful if he discovers I was the gypsy who told his fortune this afternoon."

Barbara was right.

Harry Townsend knew there was just one person in Newport who suspected him of being a thief; this person must be put out of the way. The fine Raffles preferred not to use violence, but at any cost he must win.

Harry Townsend had not recognized Bab in the gypsy tent, which served, for the time, to avert his suspicions from her. He believed she had only arrived, when he met her with Miss Stuart late in the evening. Then who was the gypsy? Either Barbara had seen her, some time in the afternoon, and told her the story of the necklace, or there was some one else who believed he had had a part in the robberies. He must find out.

"Gladys," Harry Townsend said, "don't let us dance all evening. I have not had any kind of chance to talk to you alone. Come out on the veranda with me, won't you?'"

Gladys and Harry seated themselves on the front porch, whence they could look through an open window at the dancers.

"Do you know Mrs. Cartwright very intimately, Gladys?" inquired Mr. Townsend.

"Oh, no," returned Gladys, pettishly. If Harry Townsend had brought her out on the veranda to talk about Mrs. Cartwright, then she might as well have stayed indoors. "Why do you ask?"

Harry Townsend frowned, then put his hands before his eyes. Gladys was so silly. She had served to introduce him to her friends at Newport. Now, if he could only make her useful in other ways!

"Are you angry?" Gladys asked after a moment, "What is it that you want to know about Mrs. Cartwright?"

"Oh, I don't want to know anything about Mrs. Cartwright at all, Gladys. I am sorry I spoke of it, if the subject offends you. But I did feel a little curious to know where she got hold of the gypsies she had in the tent this afternoon. I thought you would be interested."

"I am interested, Harry," declared Gladys. She was only a spoiled child, and could not help showing it. "But I am not a favorite of Mrs. Cartwright's. It's my delightful cousins that she adores—Mollie and Bab. I can ask one of them to inquire."

"Oh, no," drawled Harry, "it is not of enough importance for that."

For the next half hour Harry devoted himself to the whims of Gladys. He could see Barbara through the window, looking pale and tired. This gave all the more reason for believing that she had not recovered from the shock of her experience on the cliffs.

The cleverest man will sometimes make a false move. Harry Townsend was tired of Gladys, weary of her whims and foolishness. Besides, she had served his purpose; he was almost through with her.

"Shall we take a walk, Gladys?" he asked.

As they walked down the path toward the cliff, this up-to-date Raffles, whose fingers were more agile than a magician's, pressed Gladys's hand for a moment. At the same instant, he slipped her jeweled bracelet into his pocket. "I don't want the bauble," he said to himself, "but she might as well be punished for not doing what I ask her."

At the same moment a blond man stepped out from among the bushes and asked Harry for a light for his cigarette.

Miss Stuart and her girls were saying good-night to Mrs. Cartwright. Hugh Post and Ralph were to escort them home. As Barbara came down the steps with her wraps on, some one touched her on the arm.

"Miss," the detective whispered, "I know the man

you pointed out to me; but I have got to see you again. Tell me how we can manage it."

"Oh," said Barbara, hopelessly, "I don't know. Miss Sallie will be so angry!"

"You can't quit us now," the detective urged. "Why not come out in the morning, before any of your folks are up."

"Yes," agreed Barbara, quickly. She didn't have time to refuse. Miss Sallie was coming toward her, and looked in surprise at Barbara's strange companion. "Come on, child," she said, "it is time you and Ruth were both in bed."

"Down the street, two turnings to the right," Barbara heard a voice behind her whisper, as she turned away.

Gladys was crying, as she made her way to Miss Stuart for comfort. "Miss Stuart," she said, "I have lost my pearl bracelet. Mother told me it was too handsome for me to wear. Now she'll be angry with me. I didn't think it mattered if I wore it this one time. It was large, I suppose, and it slipped off my hand somewhere."

"Never mind, Gladys," advised Harry Townsend, coming up to her. "If it is stolen, the thief is sure to be caught."

"Why do you stare at us so, Barbara?" demanded Gladys, angrily. "I am sure you look all eyes."

"I beg your pardon," murmured Barbara.

CHAPTER XIX

"Eyeology"

All night long Bab tossed and tumbled in her bed. Should she keep her appointment with the detective? About daylight she fell asleep and wakened with her mind fully made up. Whatever the danger, she was in for it now. A clever thief was abroad in Newport; circumstances had led to her discovering him; well, she would do what she could to bring him to bay.

At six o'clock Barbara slipped quietly out of bed, without awaking Mollie, and stole noiselessly through the deserted halls of Mrs. Ewing's great house. Not even the servants were about.

At the appointed place she found waiting for her two detectives instead of one.

"We're wise to the thief," said the larger, blond man, to whom Barbara had talked yesterday. "I never had my eyes off of him last night, after you pointed him out to me. I saw him slip a bracelet from a young lady's arm out in the garden, just as coolly as you'd shake hands with a person. But it was no time to make a row then. I never let him know that I saw him. The fellow would have had a thousand excuses to make. I could see he was on pretty intimate terms with the young lady."

"The truth is, miss," interrupted the other detective, whom Bab saw for the first time this morning, "we think you have given us the clue to a pretty clever customer. We've been looking for him before. He's known to the service as 'The Boy Raffles.' We tried to catch him two years ago when he played this same game at Saratoga. But he got off to Europe without our ever finding the goods on him. So you see, this time we've got to nail him. My partner and I," the wiry little dark man pointed to the big blond one, "have been talking matters over and we believe this here 'Raffles' has got what we detectives call a 'confed' with him—some one who receives the stolen goods. So that's why we want to ask your help. Have you any idea of anyone who could be playing the game along with him? We think he is giving the jewels to some one to keep in hiding for him. The gems have not been sent out of town, and we have made a thorough search of Mrs. Erwin's house, where Townsend is staying. There is nothing there."

"Could the young lady I saw him in the garden with last night be a partner of his?" asked the blond detective.

"Oh, my goodness, no!" cried Barbara, in horror. "She is my cousin, Gladys Le Baron."

"Now, that's just it, miss. You can see we need some one like you, who's on the inside, to keep us off the wrong track. Can you suggest anyone else?"

Barbara was silent. Then she shook her head. "I

don't know of anyone now," she said. "You'll have to give me time to think and watch."

"All right, miss, and thank you. You can write a note to this address if you have anything to communicate." One of the men handed her a card with the number of a Newport boarding house on it. "My name is Burton," said the big man, "and my assistant is Rowley. We both came up from the New York office, and we're at your service, miss."

On the way home Barbara tried to make up her mind whether she ought to tell Miss Sallie what she was doing.

"I don't think it best to tell her now," she concluded. "She would only be worried and frightened to death. What is the good? Miss Sallie would be sure to think that girls did not hunt for jewel thieves in her day. And she'd probably think they ought not to hunt for them in my day," Barbara confessed to herself, honestly. "I'll just wait a while, and see how things develop. Now I am in this detective business, I might as well confess to myself that it is very interesting."

Barbara walked slowly. "I wish Ruth would find out how things are going," she thought to herself. "She is so shrewd and she already guesses I have something on my mind. But Ruth was so positive I was wrong about Harry Townsend, at Mrs. Erwin's ball, that she would probably think I was wrong again. So the female detective will pursue her lonely way for a little while longer— and then, I just must tell some one," Bab ended.

Miss Sallie and the girls were coming downstairs to breakfast, when Bab entered at the front door. Miss Stuart was plainly displeased with Barbara's explanation. "I couldn't sleep very well, Miss Sallie," said Barbara, "and I went out for a walk." "That is partly true," she reflected, "but half truths are not far from story-telling."

"Well, I must ask you, Bab," said Miss Sallie, in firm tones, "not to leave the house again in the morning, unless some one is with you. I was most uneasy."

"Didn't Mollie give you the note I left on the bureau to explain where I had gone?" inquired Bab.

"Mollie did not see the note until we were almost ready to come downstairs. Naturally, we did not understand your absence."

"I am so sorry, Miss Sallie," cried Bab. "I never will do it again."

Barbara was beginning to understand Miss Sallie better since Ruth's accident. She knew that her cold exterior hid a very warm heart.

As for Miss Sallie, she finally smiled on Bab and gave her a forgiving kiss. "I could forgive Bab anything," she thought to herself, "after her wonderful heroism in saving Ruth. I suppose I have to expect a girl of so much spirit to do erratic things sometimes."

Ralph kept his eyes lowered when he said good morning and hardly spoke during breakfast.

"Ralph is out of sorts," his mother complained, "but, man-like, he won't tell what is the matter with him."

"Perhaps you are tired from the party last night, Ralph?" suggested Mollie. Then Ralph laughed a mirthless laugh. "No, I am not tired, Mollie," he replied.

Yet all through breakfast he did not once speak to Bab.

"Remember," said Grace, "that our crowd and just a few other people are invited over to Mrs. Cartwright's to-night. She is going to have a porch party, and we are to play the famous game 'eyeology' that she was talking of to Gladys the other day. Do you know what she means?"

Nobody at the table had ever heard of it.

"I begged Donald to tell me," Grace added, "but he declares he is as much in the dark about it as the rest of us, and Mrs. Cartwright simply says, 'wait and see!'"

"I suppose," said Miss Sallie, "that you children never intend to rest again. I should think that Mrs. Cartwright would be perfectly used up from so much entertaining."

"O Aunt Sallie," pleaded Grace, "we shall rest well enough when we are back in sleepy old Kingsbridge. There is too much doing in Newport. And, you know, we've only about a week longer to stay. What a wonderful time we have had!"

"Let's see what we have ahead of us," pondered Mollie. "The only especially big things we know about are the tennis tourney and the ball after it. Then Miss Ruth Stuart and Mr. Hugh Post are to win a silver cup, in order to spread more luster upon the reputation of the automobile girls at Newport. Bab helped pull Ruth out of an abyss! The two girls held up a burglar! Ruth is a famous tennis champion! Only you and I are no good, Grace. What can we do for our country?" finished Mollie.

"Nothing at all, dear!" laughed Miss Sallie, and the rest of the party. "Much as I admire these two clever lassies, I am very glad to have my other two girls of a more peaceful and quiet variety, or my hair would certainly turn whiter than it is now, if that were possible." Miss Stuart touched her snow-white hair, which was very handsome with her delicate skin and bright color.

"Now I insist," she said, "that you girls have a quiet day if you are going out again this evening."

"May I have a row on the bay with Ralph?" asked Barbara. "Have you forgotten, Ralph, that you invited me several days ago?"

"I am sorry, Barbara," Ralph answered, quietly, "but I had forgotten it. If you will excuse me, I have something else on hand for today that I must attend to. Perhaps you will go with me some other time," he proposed, without any enthusiasm.

"All right, Ralph," Bab nodded. "Of course, I do not mind. We did not have a real engagement, anyway. He won't let me make up with him," Bab thought. "I wonder why he is so angry?"

At five o'clock Barbara came down on the veranda, dressed for the evening. She spied Ralph walking alone down the garden path, which was arched with trellises of crimson and pink rambler roses. There were several seats along the walk, and it had formed a favorite retreat for the girls ever since they had arrived at Mrs. Ewing's home.

Perhaps another girl than Barbara would not have tried again to make friends with Ralph, after his refusal to take her boating in the morning; but Bab was so open-hearted and sincere that she could not bear a misunderstanding. She was fond of Ralph, he had been kind to her, and his manner toward her had changed so suddenly that she felt she must have done something to wound him. Bab did offend people, sometimes, with her quick speeches and thoughtlessness, but she was always ready to say she was wrong and to make amends.

"Ralph!" she called. "Ralph!" The boy was obliged to stop and turn round, as Barbara was hurrying after him.

"I want to talk to you, please," she said, coaxingly. "You are not too angry with me to let me speak to you, are you?"

"I have not said I was angry with you, Miss Thurston," replied Ralph.

"Now, Ralph!" Barbara put her hand lightly on his sleeve. "You know you don't call me Miss Thurston. We decided weeks ago it was silly for us to call each other Miss and Mister when we were such intimate friends. I want you to do me a favor. Will you take me over to Mrs.

Cartwright's to-night? Donald and his guest, 'the fresh-man,' are coming for Grace and Mollie. Ruth, of course, is going over with Hugh, and I could go with them, but I want to talk to you. I can't say what I have to say to you now, because already the girls are calling me. Please say you will take me."

Barbara's eyes were so pretty and pleading that Ralph felt his anger already melting. Yet Ralph's feeling toward Barbara was not only anger. It was a much more serious thing, a growing sense of distrust. But he answered: "Of course, Bab, I shall be delighted to take you."

Barbara and Ralph let the rest of their friends start ahead of them. They wanted to have their walk alone.

Miss Sallie had pleaded fatigue, and remained at home. "Besides, children," she explained, "I am much too old to take any further interest in games, 'eyeology,' or any other 'ology.'"

Ralph and Barbara walked in silence down the street for several minutes. Then Bab spoke. "Tell me, Ralph, what is the matter? If you were angry with a man you would tell him what the trouble was, if he asked you. It is not fair not to be open with me because I am a girl. If you think you are being more polite to me by not telling me why you are angry, then I don't agree with you. I think you are acting a whole lot worse."

Ralph continued to go on in moody silence.

"All right, then, Ralph," said Barbara; "I can't ask

you any more questions, or beg your pardon, when I don't know what I have done to offend you. Only I am sorry."

"Oh, it isn't that you have offended me, Bab," Ralph burst out. "Do you suppose I would act like such a bear if you had just thrown me down, or some little thing like that, when we have been such jolly good friends before? I didn't like your sending me off yesterday, when you went to look for Mollie, because—because——"

"Go on, Ralph," insisted Barbara.

"Very well, then, Bab; I was angry and hurt because, if you did join Mollie, you couldn't have stayed with her a minute. I saw you, just afterwards, holding a long conversation with a strange man."

"Well, Ralph," argued Bab, "was that such a dreadful offense? I am sure I should not have been angry with you, if you had talked to any number of strange women." Bab's eyes were twinkling. She had made up her mind that she wanted a confidant. Here was Ralph, the best one she could have.

"That's not all," Ralph continued, "I did not mean to be an eavesdropper, but I was standing just behind you and I could not help overhearing that strange man make an appointment to meet you this morning. Say, Bab," Ralph turned toward her, all his anger gone, "don't do things like meeting that man this morning without telling. It's not nice, and I've thought you the nicest, most straightforward girl I ever knew. If there is anything between you and that fellow, why should it be a secret? A girl can't afford to have secrets, except with other girls."

"But I want to have a secret with *you*, Ralph," rejoined Barbara. "Now listen, while I tell you everything. I have never talked to you about the scene in the conservatory, the night of Mrs. Erwin's ball, though I did appreciate what you did to help me out when I made that strange request of Harry Townsend. I was not crazy. I saw Harry Townsend steal Mrs. Post's emerald necklace. Ralph," Barbara's voice was now so low that he had to bend over to hear her, "Harry Townsend is not what the people here think him. He is a professional thief, and a dangerous one."

"Whew!" whistled Ralph. "What did you say?"

Then Barbara told him the story of the three thefts, from the beginning, and her own part in discovering them. "The detectives are on the lookout now, Ralph," she added, "but they want me to keep a watch from the inside."

"Well, you are a clever one, Bab!" declared Ralph. "Look here, I am glad you told me this. I appreciate it a whole lot, and I will not mention it to anyone until you tell me I may. But, remember one thing. I shall be on the watch, too, and it's Miss Barbara Thurston I'll be watching. That Townsend is a dangerous rogue. I've known there was something crooked about him from the first. Oh, it's easy to say that, now, after what you have told me. I am not pretending I knew his special game. Only I knew he was not our sort.

He is a whole lot older than he pretends to be, for one thing."

"Ralph," sighed Barbara, "do you think there is any way I could warn Gladys against Harry Townsend?"

Ralph shook his head. "Not any way that I know of. She would just snub you hard, if you tried. Even if you dared to tell her the truth she would go right off and tell that Townsend fellow. She's been pretty hateful to you, Bab. I don't see why you should care."

"Oh, but I do care," retorted Bab. "She has been horrid and stuck up, but she hasn't done Mollie and me any real harm, and she is my cousin. Her father is my mother's brother. Uncle Ralph has never been very fond of us, nor has he come to see us very much, but he looks after mother's money. I don't suppose," wound up Barbara, thoughtfully, "he would do us any wrong. I shouldn't like Gladys to get into trouble."

"What has kept you children so long?" asked Grace, as Ralph and Barbara appeared on Mrs. Cartwright's veranda. Then she squeezed Bab's hand and whispered, so no one else could hear, "Made it up, Bab?" Barbara nodded, "yes."

Mrs. Cartwright was heard speaking. "Sit down, everyone, over there where Jones has placed the chairs for us. Professor Cartwright," she bowed to show she meant herself, "will now explain to his pupils, or his guests, the principles of the science of 'eyeology.' Human character is expressed in the human eye—our love, our hate, our ambitions, everything. But can we read the characters of people about us as we look into their eyes? No! Why not? Because the rest of the face confuses our attention. Instead of the steadfast beacon of the eye, we see the nose, the mouth, the hair, all the other features, and so we fail to understand the story the eye would tell us if it were alone. To-night I intend to instruct you in the proper understanding of 'eyeology.'"

Mrs. Cartwright changed to her usual manner of speaking. "Don't you think it would be amusing to make a test? Here Ruth," laughed the hostess, "be my first pupil. Go into the drawing-room and wait there until I send for you. I want to find out how many of your friends you will know, when you see only their eyes."

CHAPTER XX

Ruth Wakes Up!

A curious sight met Ruth's gaze when she was invited to return to the veranda.

"Goodness!" she laughed. "It is just as well I am not afraid of ghosts. I've come upon a whole army of them all at once!"

Mrs. Cartwright had the porch darkened, except for a single row of bright lights. Her visitors stood with their backs against the wall, a sheet drawn up on a level with their eyes. Another white cloth covered their heads, drawn down so low over their foreheads that even the eyebrows were concealed. By standing on books and stools the eyes were all on a level.

"No giggling," said Mrs. Cartwright severely to the ghostly set in front of her, "or Ruth can guess who you are by the tones of your voices."

Ruth looked confused. No signs of her friends remained, save a long row of shining eyes, black, blue, brown and gray, even the color being hard to distinguish in the artificial light.

"Now, mademoiselle," said Mrs. Cartwright, still

speaking in the voice of a professor, "behold before you an opportunity to prove your skill in the remarkable science of 'eyeology.' I have a piece of paper and a pencil in my hand. As you gaze into each pair of eyes, you are to reveal that person's identity. I will write the names down as you tell them to me. When you have gone through the whole list, the curtain shall be lifted. Then we shall discover how many of your friends you know by the character of their eyes. After Ruth has finished, anyone else who wishes may try his or her skill."

"My dear Mrs. Cartwright," said Ruth, laughing and peering in front of her, "I tell you, right now, that I shall not guess a single name correctly. To tell the truth, I never saw any of these eyes before. It's horrid to have them all staring and blinking at me. I am frightened at them all! Besides, I can't see. May I have a candle and hold it up in front of each person as I pass along?"

"Yes," said Mrs. Cartwright; "only kindly keep at a safe distance. We don't want to burn up any of our ghosts."

Ruth started down the line. She had the privilege of staring as long and as hard as she liked into each pair of eyes.

The company was strangely silent. They were really interested in the idea, and knew that any talking would spoil the whole experiment.

"I've mixed the babies up, Ruth," said Mrs. Cartwright, "so you needn't think you can guess anyone by his choice of a next-door neighbor. No social preferences have been allowed in this game."

Ruth tried the first pair of eyes. She looked at them intently. Then she turned round to Mrs. Cartwright. "I am sure I never saw those eyes before. You have introduced some stranger since I left the porch."

"There is not a person here whom you do not know well," Mrs. Cartwright assured her. "Don't try to slip out of your task."

Ruth kept staring. The eyes in front of her drooped, and soft, curling lashes for an instant swept over them. A little wistful look lay in the depths of them, when the lids lifted. "Why, it's Molliekins! How absurd of me not to know her! I was about to guess Ralph!"

Mistress Ruth must have guessed wrongly next time, for there was a burst of laughter, afterwards, that made the white sheets shake.

"Be quiet," warned Mrs. Cartwright sternly.

So Ruth passed on down the line. There were about twenty people in the game, but Ruth knew all of them very well. Sometimes her guesses were right, sometimes they were wrong. Once or twice she had to confess herself beaten, and "gave up" with a shake of her head at Mrs. Cartwright.

Ruth had nearly finished her task. Only a few more pairs of eyes remained to be investigated.

"Well, I am nearly through," she said gayly. "If anyone thinks I have had an easy time of it, he has only to take my place and try the next turn. No more mistakes now, for Ruth Stuart! Who is my next victim?" Ruth held her candle above her head and looked up.

Gleaming at her through the darkness lit by the flare from her candle-light was a pair of eyes that were strangely familiar.

Ruth stared at them. They belonged to none of the friends she knew—yet, somewhere, she had seen them before.

Ruth looked and looked. The eyes shifted and narrowed. Ruth still held her candle aloft; but she had forgotten where she was. Where had she seen those eyes before?

"Look straight ahead of you," said Mrs. Cartwright to the gleaming eyes, "how can Ruth guess when your eyes are closed?" But again the eyes shifted.

"I am going to find out to whom those eyes belong, if I stay here all night," said Ruth, speaking to herself.

The eyes glinted, narrowed and shone like two fine points of steel.

"Oh!" said Ruth. She staggered a little and the candle shook in her hand. "I thought I knew those eyes, but I don't. I must be mistaken. I beg your pardon, Mrs. Cartwright," said Ruth, "but I am tired. I don't think I can go on. Will some one take my place?"

Ruth's expression was so peculiar that Mrs. Cartwright came up to her. "You foolish child!" she said, putting her hand on Ruth's shoulder, "I believe this game is making you nervous. Who is it sitting there with the eyes that Ruth remembers, yet will not reveal to us?" she called.

"Harry Townsend, Harry Townsend!" the people sitting closest to him answered.

"Harry," said Mrs. Cartwright, "you come and take Ruth's place. Let's see if you are a better 'eyeologist' than she is."

Before Harry Townsend had slipped out from under his strange covering, Ruth turned to Mrs. Cartwright. "Excuse me for a minute," she begged. "My labors as an optician have used me up. I will be back in a little while."

Barbara crept from under the sheet, and, without speaking to anyone, ran after Ruth, who was on her way upstairs to Mrs. Cartwright's boudoir.

"Ruth, dear, what on earth has happened to you? Are you sick?" asked Barbara.

"Oh, I am worse than sick, Bab!" muttered Ruth, with a shudder. "Don't ask me to talk until we get upstairs."

The girls closed the dressing-room door.

"I must be wrong, Bab, yet I don't believe I am. I saw to-night the same eyes that glared at us from behind a black mask the time of that horrible burglary at New Haven, when, for a little while, I thought you were killed. I have never said much about it. I wanted to forget and I wanted everyone else to forget it, but those eyes have followed me everywhere since. To-night——"

Bab took Ruth's hand.

"Oh, Bab," groaned Ruth, "what does it mean? I saw those eyes again to-night and they were Harry Townsend's. I wanted to scream right out: 'Burglar! robber!' But I could not make a scene. I came upstairs, hardly knowing how I reached here."

One of the maids knocked at the door. "Do the young ladies wish anything? Mrs. Cartwright sent me up to inquire," she said.

"Nothing at all. Tell her we are all right, and will be down in a few minutes."

"Ruth," said Barbara, "I want to tell you something. If I do, can you pretend that nothing has happened, and be perfectly composed for the rest of the evening? Now don't say 'yes' unless you feel sure."

Ruth looked straight at Barbara, "Yes; tell me what it is," she urged. "I am beginning to guess."

"The eyes you saw to-night were Harry Townsend's, and he is a burglar and a thief. I did not know he was the robber at New Haven; I have only suspected it. Now I feel sure, and you recognized him to-night. He is a more dangerous character than I had thought, and he must not know that you suspect him."

"He shall know nothing from me," said Ruth, coolly. Her color had come back, now that she knew the truth. "It was only the shock that unnerved me. Why haven't you told me before, Bab?"

"I was afraid you'd ask me that, Ruth, dear, and I want to explain. You see, I have believed Harry Townsend a thief ever since I saw him, with my own eyes, take the necklace from Mrs. Post's neck at Mrs. Erwin's ball; but you were positive I was wrong, and asked me not to talk about it. So I didn't know what to do. I have only watched and waited. To-night I told Ralph what I knew."

Barbara then explained to Ruth the whole story, and the part the detectives had asked her to play in Townsend's apprehension. "What shall I do, Ruth?" she ended.

"Come on downstairs, Bab," said Ruth. "Some one may suspect us if we don't. Do, Bab. We are going on to play the game, just as you have been playing it by yourself. We will say nothing, but we will do some hard thinking; and, when the time comes, we shall act! To tell you the truth, if you will never betray me to Aunt Sallie, I think playing detective beats nearly any fun I know."

"Eyeology" was no longer amusing the guests when the two girls came downstairs; indeed, the company had scattered and was talking in separate groups. Ruth and Bab joined Mollie and Grace, who were standing near Mrs. Post and their new acquaintance, the Countess Bertouche.

"Girls," asked Mrs. Post, "would you like to join the Countess Bertouche and myself Saturday afternoon? We are going to explore old Newport; the old town is well worth seeing. The countess tells me this is her first visit to Newport, so, before she goes back to Paris,

I want her to see that we have a little of the dignity that age gives.

"Why," and Mrs. Post turned smilingly to the little group, "Newport boasts even a haunted house! It is not occupied, and I have the privilege of showing you over it. A story has been written about the old mansion. Here a young woman lived who loved an officer in Rochambeau's fleet, when the gallant French sailor came over to these shores. But the sailor loved and sailed away, never to return. So the lady pined and died; but her presence still haunts the old house. You can feel her approaching you by a sudden perfume of mignonette. After we see all the sights of the town, we shall go to the old house at about dusk, so that we may have a better chance to discover the 'spirit lady.'"

Mollie and Grace accepted Mrs. Post's invitation with enthusiasm. Barbara and Ruth had to decline regretfully.

"You see, Mrs. Post," Barbara explained, "Ruth and Hugh have to practice their tennis, every hour they can manage, until the tournament on Monday. Ruth has become a little out of practice since her accident, and must work hard at her game for the next few days. Ralph and I have promised to help by furnishing the opposition."

"You'll excuse Mollie and me from playing audience, won't you, Ruth?" asked Grace. "We are going home so soon after the tournament is over that we can't resist Mrs. Post's invitation."

"Barbara," said Ruth, coming into Bab's room, just as that young woman was about to step into bed, "can you imagine anyone whom Harry Townsend can be using as a confederate?"

"Sh-sh!" warned Bab. "Here comes Mollie. Don't say anything. I haven't the faintest idea."

CHAPTER XXI

The Capture of the Butterfly

Harry Townsend was not aware of the chain of suspicion that was tightening around him; but he was too clever not to use every precaution. Once or twice he had come across the small, dark detective who was making investigations in Mrs. Erwin's house—the large, blond man, named Burton, had kept in the background—but knowing that the servants had been under suspicion, he supposed that the search was being made on their account. He knew of no act of his own that could possibly implicate him in the robberies. He came and went among Mrs. Erwin's guests, and was on a friendly footing with their most fashionable friends at Newport. He had seen no one else during his visit, as the whole world was privileged to know.

The only act that the detective, Rowley, was able to report to his superior was that Mr. Townsend mailed his own letters. In Mrs. Erwin's household it was the custom of her guests to place all their mail in a bag, which the butler sent to the postoffice at regular hours; but Mr. Townsend preferred to mail his own letters.

This act occasioned no comment. Other guests, writing important business letters, had done the same thing.

"And Townsend has mailed only letters," continued Rowley in making his report. "Not a single package, even of the smallest size, has gone out through the post-office. The jewels are still in Newport."

Mr. Townsend had already begun to discuss with his hostess the possibility of his soon having to leave her charming home. "I have presumed on your hospitality too long," he said to Mrs. Erwin, several times. "When the famous Casino ball is over I must be getting back to New York."

To Gladys he explained: "My dear Gladys, my holiday time must end some day. I shall be able to see you often when you go back to Kingsbridge. I am going into a broker's office as soon as I get back to New York. I have been loafing around in Europe for the last two years, but I have decided that, even if a fellow has money enough to make him fairly comfortable, work is the thing for the true American!"

To-day Harry Townsend walked to the postoffice alone. He carried three letters. One of them was to a steamship company engaging passage to Naples for "John Brown." The steamer was due to sail the following Wednesday. The other two letters had New York addresses. When they arrived at their first destination, they were to be remailed to other addresses. A tall, blond man, who happened to be lounging in the postoffice at the time Mr. Townsend entered it, observed that the young gentleman was anxious to know when the letters would be delivered in the city.

The letters posted, Townsend walked over to the Casino courts, where Bab and Ruth were playing tennis. He had promised Gladys to join her there. He still had some investigations he desired to make. But he walked slowly. Clever fingers must be directed by a clever brain, whether their work be good or evil. No matter how well he knew he could depend on his wonderful fingers to do their share of the work, the "boy Raffles" always thought out carefully the plan of his theft before he tried to execute it.

On Monday night, at the Casino tournament ball, he planned to make his final theft. This accomplished, he could leave Newport feeling he had reaped a rich harvest, even in the summer season, when harvests are not supposed to be gathered.

Harry Townsend, alias half a dozen other names, had seen the jewel he most coveted for his final effort. It was a diamond tiara belonging to one of the richest and most prominent women in Newport. His schemes were carefully laid. He was waiting for Monday night.

At about three o'clock, on this same Saturday afternoon, Mrs. Post and the Countess Bertouche stopped in a small automobile for Grace and Mollie. They had no one with them except the chauffeur.

It took them some time to drive through the old town of Newport. The ladies descended at the old Trinity church, to investigate it, and the girls were much interested in the ancient jail. There, they were told, was once kept a woman prisoner who complained because she had no lock on her door.

Mollie and Grace were not ardent sightseers. It was really the thought of the haunted house that had brought them on their pilgrimage. But Mrs. Post and the countess insisted on poking their way down the Long Wharf, with its rows of sailors' houses and junk shops. Both girls were dreadfully bored, and secretly longed to be on the tennis courts with Bab and Ruth. Yet the thought of the haunted house buoyed them up.

Mrs. Post was a collector. If you have ever traveled with one, you will understand that it means hours and hours of looking through dirt and trash in order to run across one treasure that a collector regards as "an antique."

Even when Mrs. Post was through with her search she decided that it was not yet sufficiently late for them to visit the haunted house. "I told the caretaker not to meet us there until a quarter of seven. We shall want only a few minutes to go through the old place; but, of course, we must see it under conditions as romantic as possible." Mrs. Post then ordered the chauffeur to take them for a drive before driving them to the haunted house.

Mollie and Grace were unusually quiet, so they noticed that the Countess Bertouche had little to say during the afternoon. She seemed tired and nervous.

When Mrs. Post asked her questions about her life abroad, after she married, the countess replied in as few words as possible.

At exactly the appointed time the automobile delivered its passengers before the door of the house they sought. It was an old, gray, Revolutionary mansion, three stories high, with a sloping roof and small windows with diamond-latticed panes. It was quite dark when the girls entered the ghostly mansion, following Mrs. Post and the countess, who were led by a one-eyed old caretaker carrying a smoky lamp. There was just enough daylight shining through the windows to see one's way about, but the corners of the vast old house were full of terrifying shadows.

"Let us not stay too long, Mrs. Post," urged the countess. "I am not fond of ghosts, and I am tired." But Mrs. Post was the kind of sight-seer who goes on to the end, no matter who lags behind. She led the party up the winding steps, peering into each room as they went along. The house was kept furnished with a few rickety pieces of old furniture.

When they reached the second floor, the caretaker announced that the middle bedroom was the sleeping apartment of the haunted lady. The little party searched it curiously. There was no sign of the ghostly inhabitant; no perfume of mignonette.

"I don't see anything unusual about this room," said the countess, suppressing a sigh, "except that it has the most comfortable chair in the house. I shall sit here and rest while you take the two girls over the other part of the building."

The three left her. The woman dropped into a chair, and a worn, nervous look crossed her face.

As Mollie ascended the attic stairs behind Grace she called out, "If you will excuse me, Mrs. Post, I shall go down and join the countess."

An imp of mischief had entered Mollie. Wrapped up in her handkerchief, carefully concealed in her purse bag, was a handful of mignonette, which she had gathered from Mrs. Ewing's garden only that morning. Mollie meant to impersonate the "spirit lady." Suddenly she had decided that the countess was the best one upon whom she could try her joke.

Creeping down the stairs as quietly as a mouse, Mollie stole into the back room, adjoining the one where the countess sat. Had she looked in, she would hardly have played her naughty trick. The woman who sat there was a very different person from the gay society lady they had been meeting everywhere in the last few weeks. This woman looked weary and frightened. But Mollie was thinking only of mischief.

Silently she took the mignonette out of her bag and crushed it in her hand. There was a sudden fragrance all about her. Then she slipped her hand slyly through the open doorway and dropped her bunch of mignonette into the room where the countess was sitting. There was no response. The countess had not detected the odor of the flowers and Mollie was deeply disappointed.

Faintly, however, the countess began to be aware of the fragrance of a subtle perfume; but she was thinking too deeply of other things to be conscious of what it was. Besides, the growing darkness was making her nervous.

Mollie gave up in despair. Her effort with the mignonette had plainly proved a failure. The countess refused to be frightened by the suggestion of the ghost.

"Countess!" said Mollie, appearing suddenly in the open doorway. She certainly expected no result from this simple action; but the countess, who thought she was entirely alone, was dreadfully startled. She rose, with a short scream of surprise, and started forward. Her foot catching in a worn old rug, she stumbled. Mollie was by her side in a second, trying to help her to rise.

"I am so sorry to have frightened you!" the child said penitently. "Wait a minute, you have dropped something." Mollie picked up a square chamois skin bag. In her excitement and embarrassment she caught hold of the wrong end of it. Out of it tumbled a purse, and—Mollie saw it as plainly as could be, though it was nearly dark in the room—Mrs. Cartwright's diamond butterfly!

"Child!" said the countess, angrily. "See what your nonsense has done! This is the bag that I wear under my dress to carry my money and jewels. It is always securely fastened. I suppose, falling as I did, I must have broken the catch." She picked up the things quickly and thrust them into her bag. It was so dark in the room she supposed Mollie had not seen them. Then, holding the bag tightly in her hand, she went on downstairs, Mollie after her, and joined Grace and Mrs. Post, who had preceded them to the automobile.

"Well, did anyone see the ghost?" asked Mrs. Post. "You, Mollie, my child, look as if you had seen something."

"Oh, no," denied Mollie; "but I am afraid I frightened the countess. I threw some mignonette in the room, trying to make her think I was the ghost, but she didn't notice it. Then, when I spoke to her to tell her it was time to come downstairs, she was dreadfully startled."

Mrs. Post ordered the chauffeur to drive home first, as she and the countess had a dinner engagement; the two girls being later taken to Mrs. Ewing's.

The two women had barely left the car before Mollie put her lips near Grace's ear and whispered: "Grace Carter, the Countess Bertouche has stolen Mrs. Cartwright's butterfly! I saw it with my own eyes. She dropped it out of a bag on the floor, when she fell down."

"Goose!" smiled Grace. "What are you talking about? Don't you suppose a countess may have a jeweled butterfly of her own?"

"Not like that one," retorted Mollie, firmly. "I would know it among a thousand. You needn't believe me, but it's as true as that my name is Mollie Thurston. I am going to tell Ruth and Bab, as soon as I get home. I know they will believe me."

"I do believe you, only I am so dumfounded I can't take it in," said Grace.

"What on earth is the matter with you, Mollie?" asked Bab of her sister, as soon as they had finished dinner. "You look awfully excited."

"Bab," whispered Mollie, "call Ruth and Grace right away. Don't let anyone else come. Let's go down to the end of the garden. I have something I must tell you, this minute!"

Grace had already found Ruth, and the two came hurrying along. "No, Ralph," ordered Grace, "you can't come. This is strictly a girl's party."

"Bab," began Mollie, "you will believe me, won't you? I do know what I am talking about. This afternoon I saw the Countess Bertouche with Mrs. Cartwright's diamond butterfly. She dropped it, right before my eyes, out of the same kind of bag that Miss Sallie uses to keep her jewelry in. What can it mean?"

"Ruth!" gasped Bab. "Bab!" uttered Ruth.

The two girls looked at each other in silence. Then Bab exclaimed: "It took my Mollie to make the discovery, after all!"

"What are you talking about, Barbara Thurston? What discovery have I made?" demanded Mollie.

"Ruth, do you think I had better tell the girls?" asked Bab.

Ruth nodded, and Barbara related the principal facts of the jewel robbery. She also told the girls that she and Ruth suspected that Harry Townsend had been the robber who frightened them at New Haven. "You remember," Bab continued, "he was a guest at the hotel the same night we were, and left early the next morning. If he had one of the rooms under us, he could have climbed down the fire escape and into his own room before anyone could discover him."

But Bab kept to herself that she and Ruth were expecting another burglary, and that she, Bab, was to play a part in bringing the thief to bay. Mollie and Grace would both be terribly frightened at the thought, but it was just as well that they knew enough not to be surprised at what was to follow.

Barbara went upstairs and wrote a note to the address in Newport that the detectives had given to her. It told the story just recited by Mollie.

"Ralph," requested Barbara, sauntering slowly through the hall, "will you mail this at once with your own hands? Little Mollie has done the deed, after all. She has found the woman who receives Harry Townsend's stolen goods!"

Ralph took the letter with an exclamation of surprise and hurried off to the post.

CHAPTER XXII

The Tennis Tournament

The girls were dressing for the tennis tournament. The games were to begin at noon, and continue until six o'clock. Three hours later the annual tennis ball took place at the Casino.

"You know, Ruth," said Bab, fixing a pin in her friend's collar, as they stood before the mirror, "that the really most important thing in our whole stay at Newport is your winning the silver cup in the tournament to-day."

"Oh!" cried Ruth. "Don't be quite so energetic, Bab. You jabbed that pin right into my neck. I believe I am going to win. I can't imagine a good soldier going into battle with the idea that he is going to be beaten. Why, an idea like that would take all the fight out of a man, or a girl either, for that matter. No, Hugh and I are going to do everything we possibly can to come out winners. But, if we do, Bab, Hugh and I will think we owe it to you and Ralph. You have been such trumps about keeping us up to the mark with your fine playing."

"Nonsense, Ruth!" retorted Bab, decidedly. "All Ralph and I ask this afternoon is a chance to do some shouting for the winners. What time is the tourney on for the 'eighteen-year-olds'?"

"Just after lunch; about two o'clock, I believe. Bab, are you nervous about to-night?" Ruth asked. "Do you think there is going to be a scene at the ball? The detectives will be watching Mr. Townsend closely. They suspect that he means to make another big attempt, don't they?"

"I really don't know, Ruth," Barbara answered. "I had a short note from Mr. Burton this morning. I meant to show it to you, but I did not have a chance. It simply said: 'Thanks. The game is ours. Keep a sharp lookout!' But I want to forget the whole burglary business to-day. Tennis is the only really important thing. Hurrah for Miss Ruth Stuart, the famous girl champion!" cried Barbara, then suddenly sobered down. The two girls had been in the wildest spirits all day. Indeed, Miss Sallie had sent them into the same room to dress, in order to get rid of them.

"What is the matter, Bab?" said Ruth, turning round to look into her friend's face.

"I've a confession to make to you. In my heart of hearts, way down underneath, I am kind of sneakingly sorry for Harry Townsend. I know he is a rogue and everything that's wicked. When I think of him in that way I am not sorry for him a bit. Then the thought comes of the man who has been around with us for weeks, playing tennis with us and going to our parties, and I can't quite take it in."

"I know just what you mean, Bab," replied Ruth, reflectively. "Don't you think it must be the same idea as Dr. Jekyll and Mr. Hyde? Everyone has a good and a bad side. We can't help being sorry for the good part of a person, when the evil gets ahead of it. But, then, you and I have never really liked even the good side of Harry Townsend much. So I wonder why we both feel sorry."

"It's the woman in us, I suppose," sighed Bab.

"Ruth, come in here and let me see how you look," called Miss Sallie. She had sent up to New York for a special tennis costume for Ruth. The suit was a light-weight white serge skirt with an embroidered blouse of handkerchief linen, and the only color was Ruth's pale blue necktie and the snood on her hair, which was carefully braided and securely fastened to the back of her head.

Gowns were an important part of tournament days; indeed, the New York Horse Show seldom shows more elaborate dressing than does the annual tennis tournament at the Newport Casino.

Mollie and Barbara were the proud owners of two new gowns made by their mother for this special occasion. Bab's frock was a simple yellow dimity, and she wore a big white hat with a wreath of yellow roses round it.

"You're a baby blue, Mollie, aren't you?" asked Grace

standing and admiring her little friend. Grace had on a lingerie frock of lavender muslin and lace, and a big hat trimmed in lavender plumes.

"Well," said Mollie, making her a low bow, "lucky am I to be dressed in blue, if it means I may sit near so lovely a person as you. Fortunately, lavender and blue make a pretty color combination."

Miss Stuart had a box for the tennis tournament.

When she and the girls entered it, they found it nearly filled with roses. There were no cards except a single one inscribed: "For the Automobile Girls," for Miss Sallie was as much an automobile girl as any of the others. The girls selected the bunches of flowers that seemed most suited to their costumes. Miss Sallie and Grace immediately decided on the white roses, Mollie chose the pink ones, looking in her pale blue dress and hat like a little Dresden shepherdess.

In some one's garden a yellow rose bush of the old-fashioned kind must have bloomed for Bab. "Why!" uttered Miss Sallie, holding up Bab's flowers, from which streamed a long yellow satin bow, "I have not seen these little yellow garden roses since I was a girl. See how they open out their hearts to everyone! Is that like you, Bab? Be careful how you hold them," teased Miss Sallie; "they have a few thorns underneath, and must be gently handled."

Ruth half suspected Hugh had been the anonymous giver of the flowers, as soon as she discovered her own bunch. They formed a big ball of pale blue hydrangeas, tied with Ruth's especial shade of blue ribbon.

"See!" said Ruth, laughing, and holding them up for the other girls to admire. "Hugh was not discouraged by the fact that blue flowers are so hard to find. I wouldn't have dreamed that hydrangeas could look so lovely, except on the bush."

Ruth sat in the front of the box, waiting for her name to be called for her tennis match. She was one of the most popular visitors in Newport; nearly everyone who passed her box stopped to wish good luck to her and to Hugh.

"I have seen a good many sights, in my day," said Miss Sallie, gazing around through her lorgnette, "but never one more beautiful than this."

The grass of the wide lawns was so perfectly trimmed that it looked like a carpet of moss. Over the green there swept a crowd of laughing, happy people, the women in frocks of every delicate color. Even the sober note that men's clothes generally make in a gay throng was missing to-day, for the boys, young and old, wore white flannels and light shirts that rivaled the dresses of the girls in the brightness of their hues.

Tier upon tier of seats rose up around the tennis courts; before the first game was called every one was filled.

"Give me my smelling salts, Grace," said Miss Sallie, when Ruth and Hugh were called out to commence their game. "I shall not look at them until the set is over."

"O Miss Sallie!" declared Ralph, who had quietly slipped into Ruth's place next Barbara. "I am ashamed of you for not having more courage. I am certain they will win. We shall have two silver cups in this box in the next hour or so."

Over the heads of the great crowd Barbara could see the Countess Bertouche. She was standing near Mr. and Mrs. Erwin's box, in which sat Governor and Mrs. Post, Gladys and Harry Townsend.

For the first time in her acquaintance with them, Barbara saw Harry Townsend leave his seat and walk across the lawn with the countess. Evidently she had made some request of him. Not far off Barbara could also see a tall, blond man, with a curly, light mustache, who followed the pair with his eyes and then moved nonchalantly in their direction.

But Harry Townsend was back with his friends in a minute. He had only taken the countess to her place, so that she need not be alone in the crowd.

Ruth and Hugh were easy winners. They had no such tennis battle as they fought the day they earned the right to represent their crowd over the heads of Ralph and Barbara.

"Hurrah! Hurrah! Hurrah!" shouted the crowd.

Ruth and Hugh were standing near each other in front of the judges' stand, where the prizes were awarded.

With a low bow, Mr. Cartwright presented Ruth with a beautiful silver cup and to Hugh another of the same kind. On the outside of each cup was engraved a design of two racquets crossing each other, with the word "champion" below.

Barbara and Ruth had given up all their interest and thought to the tennis match during the day; but Ruth having won her cup, both girls' minds turned to the jewel robbery.

Except for the note Bab had received in the morning, she had had no sign nor signal from the two detectives. The Countess Bertouche, apparently as calm and undisturbed as any of the other guests, had been an interested watcher of the tournament.

The girls were late in arriving at the ball. Miss Stuart had insisted on their resting an hour after dinner, and the affair was in full swing when they entered the beautiful Casino ballroom.

"You're just in time for the barn dance, all of you," called Mrs. Cartwright. "We are going to be informal for the next half hour, at least. Come, Ruth, I insist on you and Hugh leading off. You are our special tennis champions. Wasn't it hard luck that I didn't win, when my husband was a judge?"

"Miss Thurston," said Harry Townsend, turning suddenly to Barbara, "won't you dance with me?"

Barbara's hands turned cold as ice and her cheeks suddenly flamed. She hated to dance with a man whom she knew to be of the character of Harry Townsend. Yet how could she refuse?

He looked at her coolly, and Bab saw a mocking smile

curl the corners of his lips. But he was as smooth and courteous as usual.

"He is the prince of actors," thought Bab. "I was a goose to let him see how I felt. I will show him that I know how to act as well as he does, when I am forced to it."

Barbara accepted the invitation quietly. They took their places with the two long rows of dancers extending down the whole length of the great ballroom.

The barn dance, with its merry, unconventional movement, its swinging music and grace, was generally the greatest joy to Bab. But tonight, in spite of her pretense at acting, her feet lagged. She dared not look into the face of her partner. He was as gay and debonair as usual.

When the dance was over, Townsend asked Bab to walk out on the lawn with him.

As Ruth saw Harry and Barbara walk out at the door, she turned suddenly to the stranger with whom she was talking. "Will you," she said to him, "tell Ralph Ewing I would like to speak to him at once? I want to tell him something that is very important. Please forgive my asking you, but I must see him. I will wait right here until you find him." It was five—ten minutes, before Ralph was found.

Harry Townsend meant to discover what Barbara Thurston knew. She was a young girl, still at school. He was a man approaching thirty, with a record behind him of nearly ten years of successful villainy.

Would Barbara betray herself? Would she "give the game away?"

"Miss Thurston," began Harry Townsend, politely, "as I shall be going away from Newport very soon, I want to have a talk with you. I must confess, that, since the night of Mrs. Erwin's ball, I have been very angry with you. No high-minded man could endure the suggestion you made against my honor, when you asked Hugh Post to search me, so soon after his mother's jewels had disappeared. But time has passed, and I do not now feel so wounded. Before I go away, would you mind telling me why you made such an accusation against me?"

"Mr. Townsend," said Barbara, biting her lips, but keeping cool and collected, "is it necessary for you to ask me why I made such an accusation? If it is, then, I beg your pardon. The jewels were not in your possession, certainly, when the search was made. I own I was most unwise."

"Then you withdraw the accusation?" Townsend was puzzled. He had expected Barbara to defy him, to insist he had stolen the jewels, that she had seen him in the act of doing it. He was wise enough to know that, if he could once make her angry, she would betray what she knew. He had still to discover who the gypsy was that had so strangely revealed to him her knowledge of his crimes.

Barbara's heart was beating like a sledgehammer. There was a slight movement in the nearby shrubbery. Harry Townsend wheeled like a flash. Barbara turned at the same instant. It was only a stranger who had wandered across the lawn and mistaken the path, but Barbara knew that his presence there meant eternal vigilance.

"O Mr. Townsend," she said, "the music is commencing. I would rather return to the ballroom. I have an engagement for this dance."

Harry Townsend realized he must manage to entice Barbara to a more secluded part of the Casino grounds before he could have a satisfactory talk with her.

"No," he said, "we will not go back yet, I want to talk to you. We must understand each other better, before the night is over. Come!" He spoke in a voice as cold and hard as ice and took Barbara by the wrist.

Barbara could not jerk away or call for help. She decided it was best to follow him.

"You are not running away, are you, Miss Thurston?" It was Ralph's voice calling. "I am sure Mr. Townsend will excuse you, as you have a previous engagement with me."

"Oh, certainly," said Harry Townsend, pleasantly, "sorry as I am to lose Miss Thurston's society." As Barbara and Ralph walked away, he bit his lips savagely. Then he decided to follow the tall man he had seen moving about in the shrubbery. It might be that the man suspected something. But Townsend found him ten minutes later in the smoking-room, quietly moving around among the men.

"Bab," Ruth had a chance to whisper to her later in the evening, "is it all right with you? I was desperately frightened when I saw you disappear outside with Harry Townsend. Have you noticed something?"

"What?" said Bab, gazing searchingly about her.

"Only," Ruth answered, "that the Countess Bertouche is not here this evening."

Both realized that the first card in the game had been played.

CHAPTER XXIII

Brought to Bay

One other person had noticed, with even greater interest than had Ruth and Bab, that the Countess Bertouche had failed to appear at the ball. That person was the jewel thief, Harry Townsend. He was filled with a silent rage. How dared she fail him this night of all others?

All the fellow's plans were carefully laid. The woman with the jewels he coveted sat in the ballroom; large and slow witted, she would not be quick either to discover her loss or to raise an alarm. And Harry Townsend was on friendly terms with her. Once she decided to leave the brightly lighted halls for the darkness of the grounds outside, lifting the tiara would be an easy matter. But Townsend never kept the jewels he stole in his possession ten minutes after their theft. How was he to get rid of them to-night?

It was after midnight. Many of the guests had withdrawn to the veranda; the lawns were filled with people walking about. Now Harry Townsend stood back of a row of lights that cast a deep shadow. He was talking to some acquaintances. The women were elegantly gowned, and one of them wore a beautiful diamond tiara.

Bab was standing alone in the door of the girls' dressing-room. Miss Sallie had called her in, after supper, to smooth her hair. The other girls had been with her, but they had returned to join the dancers. Bab was resting and thinking. Mollie and Grace knew nothing of what she and Ruth had on their minds. The younger girls knew that Harry Townsend and the Countess Bertouche were suspected as thieves, but they did not know that the detectives were on the alert, and that the arrest might come to-night.

Barbara was wondering if she ought to tell Gladys Le Baron what she knew. After all, Gladys was her cousin; and, as she had told Ralph, the other day, Bab felt that there ought to be a certain loyalty among people of the same blood, even when they were not fond of one another.

To-night Gladys Le Baron had been more conspicuous with Harry Townsend than ever before. Not only was she seen with him constantly, but she wore an air of conscious pride, as if to say, "See what a prize I have won!"

Gladys had passed Bab two or three times during the evening, but had pretended not to see her. Now she was coming in at the dressing-room door.

"Gladys," said Bab, timidly.

Gladys turned to her haughtily. "I would rather," she

said, "that you did not speak to me. We cannot have much to say to each other. Harry Townsend told me"— Gladys spoke so passionately and with such deep anger in her tones that Barbara stared at her aghast—"of the accusation you made against him. He made me promise not to speak of it, but I will speak of it to you. I want you to know that I shall never forgive you as long as I live, and that I shall get even with you some day. You are jealous and envious of me because we have more money, and because Harry Townsend likes me. I want you never to talk to me."

"O Gladys!" said Barbara. She was angry and hurt, but she was more frightened by the real feeling her cousin showed. Did she care for Mr. Townsend so much? Gladys was nearly eighteen, and Bab knew that ever since she was a girl of fourteen she had been brought up to think she was a young lady.

"Gladys," said Bab, firmly, "listen to me! Be quiet. I cannot tell you what I wish to say in this ballroom, to-night, among all these people, but I have something to tell you that you simply must know. Do you understand? Come to my house in the morning, and don't fail." Barbara's tones were so new and commanding that Gladys could only stare at her in silent amazement.

"Yes," she said, meekly; "I will come."

Bab's eyes were burning, and her cheeks stung with the shame of the scene between herself and Gladys. In order to be alone in the fresh air, she slipped out of the dressing-room door which opened into a side yard.

This yard had a double hedge of althea bushes which led into the back part of the Casino grounds. At the same instant that Bab left the dressing-room door, a man passed her on the other side of the hedge. He was going into the back part of the garden.

The show grounds of the Casino were in a central court. In the rear, back of the kitchens, was a long arbor covered with heavy grapevines. The man Bab followed slipped into this arbor.

When Barbara glanced into it a second later—she dared not move quickly, for fear of making a noise—there was no human figure in sight. "He has gone on down through the arbor and slipped over the fence," she thought to herself.

She was feeling her way along, trying to keep in the center path. The night was dark, and there were few stars overhead.

Suddenly, Bab gave a little shriek of terror and started back. Crouching in the darkness was a man. His back was turned to Barbara, and, if the darkness was not deceiving her, he was digging in the earth.

But Barbara's shriek roused him. "You, again!" he cried. He leaped at her, and, before she could call for help, his hand covered her mouth, and her head was pressed back.

"Don't make a noise," another voice said quietly. "My instructions were not to make a scene."

Townsend felt his own arms seized and drawn down to his sides. The big, blond man, who had interrupted his tête-à-tête with Barbara earlier in the evening, was again by his side. A smaller, dark man stood near him.

"Well, we have got you this time with the goods on you, or pretty close to you," said the smaller detective, striking a match and looking down at his feet. Just near where they stood, only partially concealed by the dirt, which had been hastily dug up, something brilliant flashed and sparkled.

"Did you think, Mr. Townsend," laughed Detective Burton quietly, "that you were the only clever person in Newport? These jewels you have just stolen are hardly worth the risk you ran. You might get about twenty-five dollars for the lot. I suppose you didn't know, since it has become the fashion to have a jewel thief in Newport, it has also become the fashion to wear paste jewels." The man held the tiara in his hand. "But I will restore them to the rightful owner," he said. "Mrs. Oliver informed me they were gone, two minutes after you slipped them out of her hair."

Townsend had not spoken. "Don't," he now said, with a shudder, "put those handcuffs on my hands. I will go quietly. I see the game is up—thanks to you!" He turned to Barbara with a snarl. But Ruth and Ralph were standing close by her side.

Barbara was much shaken and frightened by her encounter, but she tried to summon a little of her old spirit. "You do me too much honor, Mr. Townsend," she answered quietly.

"Where is the Countess Bertouche?" asked Townsend stolidly.

"She is ready to leave Newport with you to-night. Only we persuaded her to get ready a little earlier; indeed, we called upon her this afternoon, while she was at the tournament, and were waiting for her when she got back. She had two or three little trinkets in her possession, which she was holding for you, that we wished to return to their rightful owners. The lady will be able to travel as soon as you are. We think it best not to have any excitement in Newport. By the way," went on the detective—the three young people were listening breathlessly—"the lady is not such a cool customer as you are. She confessed that she was not a countess, but a poor newspaper woman out of a job, whom you enticed down here to help you. She explained that you had been mailing letters of instruction to her by sending them on to New York and having them remailed to her here. A poor business it has been for both of you, I am thinking."

"Ruth," said Barbara, quickly, "it's too awful! Let us go back to Miss Sallie!"

CHAPTER XXIV

Good-Bye to Newport

Early next morning Ruth and Barbara made full confession to Miss Sallie. Mollie and Grace were not surprised, for they had been told enough of the circumstances to expect the outcome. But imagine Miss Sallie!

"You mean to tell me, Ruth and Bab," she gasped, dropping limply into the nearest chair, "that Harry Townsend is the jewel thief, the Newport Raffles? Why, you girls have walked with him, talked with him, played tennis with him! And Barbara has suspected him all the time! My heavens!" she wailed, in despair. "Did it never dawn on you, Barbara, that you might have been killed?"

Miss Stuart was overcome. "Ruth Stuart, my own niece, do you mean to tell me that you lately discovered that 'this Townsend' was the thief who tried to rob us in New Haven? Why was I not told at once? But then, I am grateful I was not. And you, Mollie, fourteen-year-old Mollie, you found out this wretch's accomplice, and discovered Mrs. Cartwright's stolen butterfly! I never would have thought it of you!"

"But I didn't mean to, Miss Sallie. It was all an accident. I am awfully sorry for that poor woman," answered Mollie.

"Nonsense, child!" said Miss Sallie. "I am grateful enough that such dangerous people are out of the way."

The girls were standing in a circle round her. "Come to my arms," she demanded of Grace. "Thank heavens, child, you have not turned detective, and can be relied on to keep me company!"

"But it was just as much Grace's fault as it was mine that I discovered the butterfly," argued Mollie, who could not see that Miss Sallie was joking. "She was with me when I found it out." Everyone joined in the laugh at Mollie's expense.

"Some one to see you in the library, miss," announced Susan, the parlor maid. "She says she'd like to see you alone, first, and she'd rather not give her name."

"Then you are not to go one step, Barbara Thurston," said Miss Stuart in the voice the girls knew had to be obeyed. "There is no telling who it is waiting for you, nor what her intentions may be toward you. You'd go if you thought you'd be murdered the next minute. I never saw a girl like you. I will go myself," announced Miss Sallie.

"Oh, no," said the girls, all pulling together at her skirts.

Miss Sallie had to pause. "If you think, young ladies," she said, calmly, "that, because I have not unearthed a jewel robber, nor attacked a burglar in the dark, I am therefore more of a coward than a parcel of silly girls, you are vastly mistaken. Let go of me!" Miss Sallie marched majestically forward.

"Susan, *I* will go down."

"Oh, no'm," pleaded Susan, giggling. She had no idea what all the fuss was about, but she knew it was most unnecessary. "Please'm, let me whisper to you. It's only that Miss Gladys Le Baron, but I promised not to give her name. I am sure she means no harm, miss. She looks like she was worried and had been crying a bit, ma'am."

"It is all right, Barbara," said Miss Sallie. "From what Susan tells me you may go downstairs alone."

Bab had not the faintest idea who could be waiting for her. In all the excitement, she had entirely forgotten that she had told Gladys Le Baron to come to see her this morning without fail. As soon as she opened the library door, she remembered. "Good morning," she said, coldly.

But Gladys flung her arms about her neck and burst into a torrent of tears. "I know it all, all!" she said. "Mrs. Post and Mrs. Erwin called me into their rooms last night, and told me everything. I had expected Harry Townsend to take me home from the ball, and, when he didn't put in his appearance, I was so angry and behaved so badly Mrs. Post said I had to be told at once.

Mrs. Erwin wanted to wait until morning. O Bab, I didn't sleep a wink last night!"

"I am sorry," said Bab, but she didn't really show a great deal of feeling.

"Bab," Gladys went on, "I simply can't believe it! And to think you knew it almost all the time! Mrs. Post says I have to believe it, now, because the whole story is out. She says she was completely deceived, too, and can understand why I thought Townsend was a gentleman. Father seemed to think he was all right. He told us all about his being an orphan, and who his rich relations were. Mrs. Erwin is so good. She just says she is sorry for me, and hasn't uttered a word of blame. Only think, I brought that dreadful wretch to her house, and I am responsible for all the trouble! O Barbara, I can never face it!" Gladys wiped her eyes again with her handkerchief, which was already wet with her tears.

"I want to go home to mother to-day, but Mrs. Erwin says I have to stay with her a little while longer. She says that, if I rush right off now, if I disappear the very same day Harry Townsend and that woman leave, people will believe there is more between us than there really is. There wasn't anything exactly serious, though I did like him. I am sure I shall never hold up my head again."

"I wanted to warn you sooner, Gladys; believe me, I did," answered Barbara; "but I knew you wouldn't listen to me, and would not believe a word I said."

"I know, Barbara," said Gladys, humbly. "I have been

a horrid stuck-up goose. I know, now, if you hadn't seen him steal the necklace at Mrs. Erwin's, we might never have found out who the thief was. Then I don't know what dreadful thing might have happened to me, if I had gone on seeing him and never understood his true nature. Do you think he could have stolen my bracelet?"

"I know he did," Bab answered.

"The horrid, hateful thing!" cried Gladys, with a fresh burst of tears. "Barbara, I want to ask you a favor. Will you beg Ruth to let me go back to Kingsbridge in the automobile with you? I suppose I ask you because I have been more hateful to you than to anyone else. I know if you will forgive me the other girls will. Ruth will do anything you ask her."

"But I can't ask Ruth such a favor as that, Gladys," argued Barbara. "There wouldn't be room in the car, for one thing."

"Oh, I could sit on the little seat and I would be as nice and give as little trouble as I possibly could, if you will only ask her. I somehow feel that if you girls will stick by me, now, other people will not think so badly of me. They will know I have been a goose, and have been dreadfully deceived by Harry Townsend, but they'll understand that I never meant any wrong, and am not really bad. You see, Bab, you and Mollie are my cousins. Everyone is sure to find out you helped to expose the awful villain; so, if I am seen with you now, it will show that you take my part, and that you knew I had only been deceived."

"Don't you think it is a good deal to ask of me, Gladys?" said Barbara, speaking very slowly. She was thinking of every snub, every cruel thrust Gladys had given her since they were children.

Gladys did not answer at first. Then she shook her head, and rose to go. "Yes, Barbara," she said; "I know I don't deserve a bit of kindness at your hands. I have been perfectly hateful to you, always. Good-bye."

"Oh, stay, Gladys," begged Bab, penitent in an instant. "I didn't mean that. Of course we will all stand by you. Indeed, I shall ask Ruth if you may go back in the automobile with us, and I am sure, if Miss Stuart thinks there is room enough, Ruth will be delighted to have you. She is always the dearest, most generous girl in the world," said Bab, her face glowing with the enthusiasm she always felt in speaking of Ruth.

"Now," she continued, "do come on upstairs and take off your hat. You must stay to lunch with us. Oh, no; you needn't be afraid of Miss Stuart. She won't be unkind to you; she's a perfect dear! She'll just be awfully sorry for you, when you tell her how badly you feel. Come on, Gladys." Bab took hold of her hand.

"Won't you call Ruth down first?" urged Gladys. "I feel too much ashamed to go right on up there among all of you."

Ruth and Bab, between them, persuaded Gladys to go to their rooms. To their surprise, Mistress Mollie was the one to be appeased. She was not so ready to kiss and make up as Bab had been, yet even Mollie's "hard" little heart softened when she saw what a changed and chastened Gladys the girls brought upstairs with them.

"You'll see I am going to be different," Gladys said to Bab, "and if ever there's a chance for me to prove how I appreciate your being so kind to me now, I shall do it. Of course, I don't expect you to have much faith in me yet."

"Miss Barbara Thurston is requested to spend her last day in Newport as the guest of honor of Governor and Mrs. Post on board their yacht, the 'Penguin,' which is at this instant awaiting her answer outside in Narragansett Bay," said Ruth, with a flourish of a letter she held in her hand and a low bow to Barbara.

"Goose!" shot Barbara at Ruth. "But are we all invited for a sail? How jolly!"

"I am no goose, madam," retorted Ruth. "I mean what I say. Read this."

She handed Barbara a letter which Miss Stuart had received from Mrs. Post only a few minutes before, and which read:

My dear Miss Stuart,

We want, in some quiet fashion, to show our appreciation of, and thanks to, the little girl who so patiently and cleverly kept her own counsel, and so materially aided in the discovery of the jewel thief. I feel that I did not do her justice. Governor Post and I both believe that it is to her wit and courage that I owe the return of my emerald necklace. I have talked matters over with Hugh, and, with your consent, I should like to give a luncheon, in her honor, on board the yacht at one o'clock to-morrow. We will spend the afternoon sailing in the bay. Only our intimate friends will be invited and we feel that no party could be complete, at Newport, without the presence of "The Automobile Girls."

Faithfully yours,

KATHERINE POST.

"What larks!" cried Barbara, blushing with pleasure. "Has Miss Sallie said we could go?"

"Certainly she has," rejoined Ruth. "I told Hugh so at once."

Columbia, the gem of the ocean,
The home of the brave and the free,
The shrine of each patriot's devotion——

The young people were in the bow of the yacht when the music commenced. "Why, Hugh," Bab whispered to him in an undertone, "have we a band on board? How perfectly delightful!"

"Young Miss America," Hugh answered, "you needn't think, for one minute, that this party on the 'Penguin' is going to enjoy any ordinary entertainment to-day. The band is not half. Just you wait, and see all the remarkable things that are to take place on this blessed boat excursion."

Earlier in the day, when Ruth and Grace first came aboard, they passed through the salon on their way to the upper deck. Grace caught hold of Ruth's sleeve and drew her back to whisper to her: "Has it ever occurred to you that Harry Townsend might have stolen your fifty dollars that disappeared after we spent our first day on the yacht? I have been thinking that he must have been dreadfully hard up, or he never would have tried the robbery at New Haven, or have stolen such a small sum from you afterwards."

"Yes, I have thought about it," said Ruth, shaking her head, with a forlorn gesture. "Isn't it too dreadful? Let's forget all about him to-day."

The luncheon was announced promptly at one.

"'The Automobile Girls,' including Miss Sallie, will kindly stay on deck until they are summoned," called Mrs. Post, sweeping on ahead, followed by her other guests.

Miss Sallie and the girls waited in some excitement. The sun was shining gayly on the deck of the little ship, which sailed through the water like a white bird. All the flags were flying in Barbara's honor, as the governor explained, when she came on board.

Suddenly Hugh's smiling face appeared at the open door. "Come in, now," he requested.

Miss Sallie and the girls marched into the long salon dining-room, while the band played "Liberty Bell."

In the center of the luncheon table, raised on a moss-covered stand, was a miniature automobile. In it

sat five dolls wearing automobile veils of different colors and long dust coats. Two of the dolls were blondes, the other two were brunettes. But the stateliest and handsomest doll of the lot had soft, white hair and reclined against a violet cushion. A pale blue flag flew over the car. It bore the inscription: "The Automobile Girls—Long May They Flourish!"

At either end of the table stood Hugh's and Ruth's silver cups, won at the tennis tournament.

As Miss Sallie and the four girls took their places, Hugh raised one cup, his mother the other. "We will drink from these loving cups," he said, "to the health of our guests of honor, 'The Automobile Girls.'" He then passed the cups, filled with a fruit punch, around the table.

At the close of the luncheon, Hugh again rose to his feet.

"Ladies and gentlemen," he announced, "I am going to make a speech."

"Don't do it, Hugh," laughed Ralph.

"All right, Ralph," said Hugh; "I won't. Barbara," Hugh leaned over to attract her attention, and Barbara turned a rosy red, "here's a souvenir of Newport for you. I guess it's a gift from us all." He motioned to his friends around the table and handed to Bab a small green velvet box. "For the girl who is always on the watch," he ended.

Barbara's eyes were full of tears. They came partly from embarrassment, but most of all from pleasure.

Inside the velvet case was a tiny gold watch, set in a circle of small emeralds.

But Mollie was calling Bab to look at her gift. Mrs. Cartwright, who sat next her favorite of the girls, had pinned a little, pearl butterfly in the lace yoke of Mollie's gown. Ruth and Grace were each rejoicing in their gifts, silver pins representing tennis racquets, their souvenirs of the luncheon and their month's stay in Newport.

"It has been just too lovely!" said Mollie to Mrs. Post, as she bade her good-night. "Yes, we start for home the first thing in the morning. In a few days there will be no more 'Automobile Girls,'" she ended with a sigh.

"Oh," said Ruth, laughing and coming up beside her, "who knows? You never can tell! Good-bye, everyone," she said, taking hold of Bab's hand. "We have had the time of our lives, just as we hoped we would. Till we meet again," she finished with a smile.

The four girls ran down the gangplank and rejoined Miss Sallie.

As many of our readers will guess, the return to Kingsbridge did not bring an end to the adventures of the natural and charming girls in their automobile. Further adventures and a host of new things remain to be told, but these must be deferred for narration in the next volume, which will be entitled, "THE AUTOMOBILE GIRLS IN THE BERKSHIRES; or, The Ghost of Lost Man's Trail."

[THE END]